God's Network

Jeff Davis series book 3

Tim Koop

This book is dedicated to

Rick Joyner,

for that quote at the end.

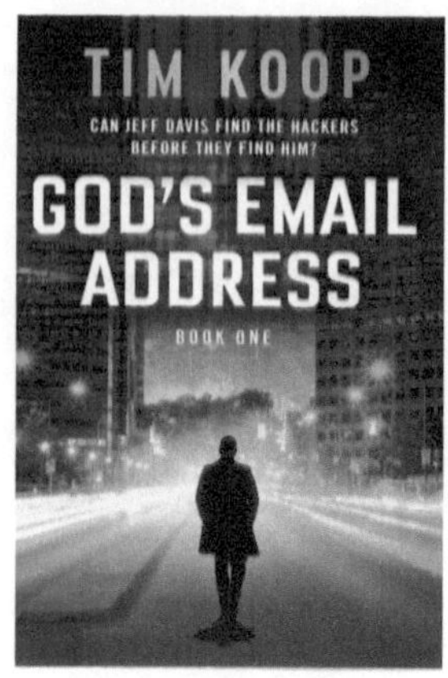

God's Email Address

Corporate email servers are being hacked. Private information is sold to the highest bidder. And they're blaming the software company.

A shy computer programmer tries to stop the corporate espionage before the men with guns stop him, permanently.

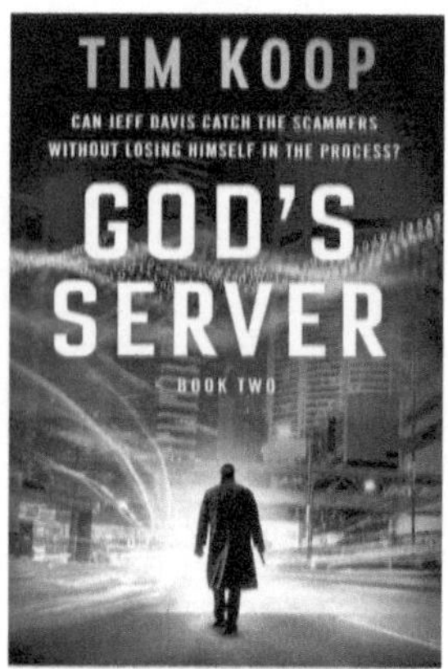

God's Server

Scammers are on the loose and nobody is safe, not even Jeff's mom.

But when this shy computer programmer tries to catch the bad guys, he finds there is more standing in his way than he realizes.

God's Network

Someone is trying to kill Jeff Davis, and succeeds.

This shy software developer has put so many bad guys behind bars, that he has made enemies, and now he is being hunted.

PRAISE FOR TIM KOOP'S WRITING

"Interesting"
 - almost everyone

"Good writing. Good action and suspense."
 - Cynthia A. Robison

"Well paced... the technical aspects were accurate... the story was interesting... I want to read the next one."
 - Thomas Sewell, editor

"It was very interesting and held my attention. You did a nice job of developing the characters and making them believable. The plot developed quite well also."
 - Jenn Haslam

"It's great!"
 - 17 year old young man, after staying up till 4:30am to finish the book

"I just finished reading [God's Email Address] and I love it! First, it is a great story that kept me involved from beginning to end. The contemporary themes were totally relatable. The story arch is very well done and the characters were well-developed and recognizable."
 - Patti Virkler

"This could be the best book I've ever read in my life."
 - Tim Koop

PROLOGUE

To avoid suspicion, the two assassins held hands, pretending to be out on a date. But they weren't dating. She worked for him. And he wasn't an assassin for hire, either. He just killed people. And after what this target had done, he deserved to die.

Car bomb instructions are surprisingly hard to find on the surface web, but when you dig a little deeper into the dark web, everything is available to you. All you need is a wireless radio controller, a blasting cap, a battery to power it, and some explosive material. These materials were purchased locally, and for a reasonable price, even though the killer didn't need to be frugal. He already was a millionaire several times over.

Most of his wealth came from illegal activity, and a lot of that had dried up because of one man. That's why that one man had to die. Nothing personal. He was just bad for business. Most rich people would hire out a job like this, but this man wasn't normal.

Stopping next to a silver Mercedes-Benz C300 Coupe, the murdering millionaire dropped to a knee as if to tie his shoe which was already tied. When he did, his backpack fell off his back and onto the ground. He quickly pushed it underneath the car, directly under the driver's seat.

"I can see it," the woman whispered loudly while glancing around.

"What?"

"I can see it. He'll notice it."

The man scowled and pushed it farther in. "How's that?"

She glanced down. "Fine."

The man started unzipping the backpack to get at the switch that armed it when the woman said something again.

"You're mumbling," he said. "Talk louder."

"I said someone's coming!"

The man quickly armed the car bomb and got up. They held hands and started walking away when the person who was coming drew near. She had a dog.

The man, displaying absolutely no remorse for what he had just set in motion, beamed at the animal. "I love dogs!" he gushed and walked over. "What kind of dog is this?"

The lady smiled. "It's a Shiba Inu."

"Ha! He looks just like the Internet."

"That's why I got him."

The killer scratched the dog behind the ears. "Are you a good boy, good boy? Yes you are." Then he stood up. "Beautiful dog you have there."

"Thanks," she responded, and kept on walking.

They continued retreating when the assistant remarked, "You love dogs but kill people?"

He scowled again. "It's a weakness of mine."

She smirked. "Killing?"

"Dogs! Loving dogs!"

"Love isn't a weakness."

This made him stop in his tracks. Then he stared at her until she became flustered. "What?" she demanded.

He pointed in her face. "You have a lot to learn." He gestured around him. "Everyone has a lot to learn. Love is not just a weakness. It is the greatest weakness of all. When you love something or someone, it is a point of vulnerability. It's like a ring in the nose of a bull. He would otherwise be a strong animal, but with a little ring, a little love, he becomes weak. He can no longer do what he wants to do. He moves from being the master to the slave. All because of love. I'll show you what to do with love. I'll show everyone."

Even though his assistant had a seed of love in her, she had seen enough pain in her life related to love to believe that this just might be true. "Well, you won't show this guy."

"Why not?"

"Because he'll soon be dead."

He stared at the Mercedes for a long time. "You have the remote detonator?"

"Yes. Why?"

"Change of plan."

CHAPTER 1

Tuesday, 8:18 PM

Scott Stark jumped out from behind a bush, aimed his pistol at Garth, and fired five times. Two bullets missed, but three hit their mark, wounding his fellow programmer severely. "Ha! Gotcha!"

"Dastardly move, Stark!" spat Garth, as he fled as fast as he could. Scott chased him at a sprint over level terrain, up steep hills, and down into holes and caves in the earth.

But as Scott chased Garth from one direction, Doug hunted him from the other. As soon as Garth was in range, Doug lobbed a grenade at him. It missed, but took out Scott completely, killing him instantly.

"Doug, you're supposed to be on my side!" Scott moaned.

"Sorry, Scott. I missed."

"Where are you guys, even?" I mumbled out loud.

"Near the left!" replied Garth and Doug.

"Not me," said Scott. "I reappeared near the middle, I think. And I see you, and I'm coming to get you."

I spied Scott coming at me from the left, so I pressed my right arrow key as hard as I could. Unfortunately for me, Scott could run faster than I could, just because he was a better player than I was, and soon he had taken me out with a few grenades. My character died, and soon reappeared on another part of the map. I sighed. I hated dying. I was getting tired of dying so often. If I ever die again, it will be too soon.

A grenade exploded in front of me, taking half my life. Did I mention I was getting tired of explosions, too? Real life isn't nearly so interesting. There weren't any explosions when you're computer programming all day long.

"Jeff Davis," Garth said to me. "Are you guarding our flag, or are you going for their flag?"

"Um...," I replied. "I guess I'll try guarding." I ran my character out to where our flag was supposed to be.

"Then do that. They've captured it several times already."

"And we have it now, too!" Scott beamed. "Yeah! And we just delivered it!" Our screens suddenly changed from the game to the scoreboard. It was pretty close. Garth was such a good gamer that he made up for my complete lack of talent, but we were still losing.

Garth took another swig of Dr. Pepper, then another bite of pizza. He didn't seem very happy. "What's it like to be losing, Garth?" Scott asked.

"Quit your bragging, Stark. We all know why we're losing."

Doug came to my rescue. "Jeff isn't doing that bad."

Garth guffawed. "This was his idea. He could at least have practiced first."

"That wouldn't have been fair," I replied.

"It would have made it more fair," he replied.

"Thanks for thinking of us, though," Scott beamed. "But why did you call this games night, anyway? Just to hang out?"

Yes, why did I? Instead of answering, my heart grew weak and I had to control my breathing. "Well..." I tried to say the words that I had practiced for weeks, but they wouldn't come out. It just took too much courage. "I..." I tried again, then gave up. "Just to hang out," I answered, then breathed a sigh of relief. "Maybe I'll get some more coffee." I stood.

"It's too late for coffee," Scott said. "You won't sleep."

"OK, some Pepsi then." I went to fill my cup with liquid

sugar.

"As you enjoy your non-Dr. Pepper beverage, can we be done this exercise in frivolity?" Garth asked. "I have things that need doing."

I shrugged. "Sure."

"Thanks for the games night, Jeff," said Scott.

"Yes. Good games, everyone," followed Doug.

"Yeah," I said, as I started packing up pizza boxes, and empty pop cans, and crushing them into a garbage can. I had failed. I had organized this event for one purpose, and one purpose only, and I had failed at it. I didn't know what I was going to do. Maybe my girlfriend Cheryl has an idea. She always has good ideas for me.

We had been playing computer games in our office at Omniscient Technologies, where we worked as software developers. Omniscient occupied most of the third floor of a downtown building. We locked the main door and headed toward the elevator.

"I've got a date coming over this evening," said Scott. It seems he was always dating someone new. Not me. I had a girlfriend Cheryl, and she was a keeper.

Soon we were on the ground, then walking to the parking lot to get in our cars. Garth went out to the parking garage and the rest of us three continued on to the outdoor parking.

I just said "Good night" to Scott and Garth for the last time and made my way towards my car. Then it exploded.

9:01 PM

I was thrown to the ground and instinctively curled up in the fetal position with my head in my hands. I didn't know what was happening, but my reflexes told me to cower and hide.

When I recovered enough that I could look around, my car

was smoking, and in ruins. There was a hole where the driver's seat was, and the vehicles on either side were damaged, too. I expected the anti-theft alarm to be sounding, but it wasn't. The blast must have taken out the battery.

Soon Scott was helping me up, and the other guys were there too, gawking. "Was that your car?"

"Yeah," I nodded, still trying to catch my breath.

"Jeff, someone just tried to kill you!"

"Yeah," I repeated, letting the thought sink in. It was still scary, even though it wasn't the first time. A few months ago I got entangled with some bad guys, but I was hoping we were done with that. I groaned. Not again.

Suddenly I glanced around in panic.

"What?" asked Doug.

"I just thought he might still be out there"

"Who?"

"The guy who did this."

I looked around frantically, but couldn't see anyone. Well, that wasn't true. I saw lots of people. People were starting to stare. There was even one man still on the ground. He must have been blown over by the blast, too. He hobbled out to us. "Dude, that wasn't your car, was it?"

"Yeah," I nodded.

He ran his hand through his blond hair. "Someone tried to kill you! Who would do that?"

I didn't answer.

He continued. "And what did you do to tick someone off that bad?"

"Nothing!" I replied, then added, "Well..." I started walking. I just needed to stretch my legs.

"Someone should call the police," said Doug, then he added, "I'll do it." He pulled out his phone, and started dialing.

Scott asked me, "How's your head?"

"Fine," I replied, as I turned around, and walked back.

People were starting to gather.

A lady called out, "Was anybody hurt? Was somebody in there?"

"Nobody was hurt!" Scott announced.

"Oh thank God!" she said. "What happened?!"

"Probably a car bomb."

"In who's car?"

I turned and walked away again. I didn't want to be involved in this.

The man with the blond hair answered, "It was his car!" and pointed at me.

I said, "Scott, would you like to get your car so I can sit in it and not have to be part of this crowd?"

"You bet," he said, and ran off for his Mustang.

"The police are on their way," said Doug.

Soon Scott's car was near, and the three of us got in. As soon as I had buckled my belt, the blond man knocked on my window. I looked up at him. "Open the window!" he yelled.

I cranked it down a little.

He said, "In case you need a witness, I was a witness. I saw your car explode."

"Thanks," I said, then started rolling up the window again.

"My name's Larry."

"Hi."

"What's your name?"

I sighed. "Jeff."

"Jeff what?"

"Jeff Davis."

"I'll tell the police it was your car that exploded."

"OK"

I rolled up the window. I was already feeling bad for losing the games night, then failing to accomplish what I was trying to do with the whole party. And now my car exploded. I didn't feel like doing anything else. I said, "Here's an idea. Let's go home. Scott, will you take me home, please?"

"The police are on their way," Doug responded from the back seat.

"I'll come in tomorrow morning."

"I would stay," said Doug.

But Scott said, "Why not go home? What are they going to do? Arrest you?"

"Yeah. Ha, ha," I spoke, but I didn't feel very happy about it, because a few months ago I did get arrested. That wasn't very fun at all, and I didn't feel like talking to the police again.

"OK, done. We're going home," said Scott. He dropped Doug off near his car, and then we drove away. On the way out, a police car passed us coming in. Scott waved to them, like the goofball he is, but I hoped to myself we wouldn't get in trouble. I hated getting in trouble.

9:57 PM

At home, I got out, and Scott's cherry red Mustang roared away.

I lived on the second floor of a three-story apartment. I walked up the steps in front of the building, then beeped myself in. As I got out the key to my door, the first door on the left, I heard my name.

"Jeff! Hey! Jeff!"

I looked up and groaned inwardly. It was the blond guy from the parking lot. He came and stuck out his hand. "It's me. Larry."

I shook his hand. "Hi, Larry."

"I had no idea you lived here! Imagine this. Wow."

"Yeah. You live here, too, huh?"

"Yup. Just moved in. I guess we're neighbors."

"I guess so."

"Hey, you're not hurt from the explosion, are you?"

"No, I'm fine."

"That's good to hear. I'm good, too. Hey, what do you do for work?"

"I'm a computer programmer."

"Really? I'm a computer security specialist. I'm a consultant for hire, so if you ever need a security consultant, let me know." He handed me a card that said, "Larry Trilbert, Systems Security Consultant."

I said, "Thanks."

"And you'll suggest me if it comes up?"

"Yeah, of course," I lied.

"Maybe your company needs a security specialist right now."

I thought about it. We could sure use a security specialist. We were dealing with lots of potentially sensitive information, and we did almost get hacked a while ago. I sure wasn't that great with security. Maybe Garth was, but that's it. Maybe I should suggest it to Nigel. But then again, that would mean working with this guy, not that I had anything against him, I suppose. I just don't like people in general.

"No, I don't think we do," I replied.

"OK, well, keep me in mind. Thanks, Jeff!!" He smacked me on the shoulder as if I were his good buddy. He was probably trying to be friendly, but I found it awkward. "Have a great night! I'll see you later."

He turned around and unlocked his way into number 203 down the hall. I sighed and opened up 201. It seems we were neighbors.

Before I got my shoes off, my phone rang.

"Hi, this is Jeff."

"Jeff, this is Mom." She sounded worried. "How are you?"

"Fine."

"I just heard that there was an explosion at The Forks. A car exploded, and I thought it was a kind of car you dove. It wasn't yours, was it? I wouldn't be able to sleep knowing it was your car. Jeff, tell me that wasn't your car."

I hesitated, but not very long. "Of course not, Mom. I'm fine."

"Oh, good. I was so worried. I just had to call and ask."

"That's OK. But I'm fine, Mom. You don't need to call."

"Of course not. I guess I worried for nothing. OK. Good." I heard her take a deep breath and let it out. "In that case, have a good night."

"Thanks. You, too."

"Bye."

"Bye."

For some reason, I had a bad feeling in my stomach. I suppose that happens when your car blows up, but it got really bad there when I was protecting my mom from worrying about me. Or was it Larry? I didn't understand it. Maybe if I ate something it would go away.

I wandered through the kitchen, looking for something to snack on, when I remembered that I was still full from pizza, so I didn't eat anything. But still, something didn't feel good inside of me. Maybe the feeling was left over from when I almost died. That must be it.

I got ready for bed, and then did what I did every night before going to sleep. I took out my wireless keyboard from beside my bed, and connected it to my phone. Then with the phone and keyboard in front of me, on my blanket, I started typing.

"Hello, God. It's me again, Jeff."

A while ago at work, a lady I didn't know handed me a piece of paper and she said it was God's email address. Then she said I could send God an email and he would respond. I immediately dismissed her as being crazy, because such a thought is, indeed, very crazy. But then I tried it, and I got a response. For a few days, this God and I talked. It rocked my life. A while later, I finally gave in, and surrendered to this God. His unconditional love for me did me in. Now I am his.

And in the meantime, I have learned the skill of communicating with him without an email address. After typing "Hello," I closed my eyes and pictured him next to me. When some thoughts popped into my head, I wrote them down.

"Hi, Jeff. It's always good to meet with you."

Then I wrote down words of my own. I didn't know how to be very spiritual, so I just made conversation.

"How are you?"

More words came to me, so I typed them in.

"Large and in charge. How are you, my friend, Jeff Davis?"

"I'm fine."

"Are you?"

"Maybe not. My car got bombed. I almost died. I might want to see you face to face one day, but maybe not quite yet."

"You'll see me soon enough, but you're not done down here yet."

"What would you like me to do?"

"I want you to open your heart to me. Let me love you, my son. Let me pour my love into your life. I love you, Jeffery. I love you my son, my friend."

I paused with my eyes closed. I sat there, swimming in the feelings of it all. I have been accused of not having feelings, but it's not true. There is something about spending time with this God of love that has a way of setting free the emotions of the heart.

And speaking of emotions of the heart, just then my phone rang. It was my girlfriend, Cheryl, the same person who gave me God's email address in the first place.

"Hey, Sweety!" I answered.

"Jeff, I just heard that a car exploded in the parking lot."

I sighed. I was feeling so good, now we're back to this.

"You heard about that, huh?"

"Was it your car?"

"Yup. My car. It went boom."

"Jeff, don't joke about this. You could have been seriously injured."

"Or worse."

"You mean death? No, I don't think that's going to happen."

"It could. If I would have been in it..."

"Please don't even talk about that. But you could have been hurt."

"OK, I could have been hurt, or killed."

"I don't want you to get hurt. Have you talked to the police, yet?"

"I will tomorrow."

"Hey, how are you going to get to work?"

"You want to give me a ride?"

"Sure. We can talk more then. Good night, Jeff."

"Good night, Cheryl. I love you."

"I love you too. Bye."

"Bye."

I hung up the phone. I liked her.

I journaled a bit more, then went to sleep for real. As I was drifting off to sleep, I remembered the last time I was at a police station. I had been arrested for brandishing a weapon. Tomorrow, I'll have to go back there, and talk with the same people who arrested me, to report my car. I wasn't sure I wanted to do that.

Wednesday, 7:55 AM

My favorite part of arriving at work with Cheryl was taking the elevator to the third floor with just her, because I could give her a nice good morning kiss before the doors opened.

That's a good way to start the day.

Through the front glass doors, and then through the lobby, I walked her to her cubicle, then continued to my room, which was a room in the corner of the building. The four of us developers sat there. Garth Fonte was the senior developer, and I admit he was pretty good. He was also a large man who enjoyed his Dr. Pepper. I suppose he also had a sense of humor, because he kept a joke-of-the-day posted on his little whiteboard. This morning it said, "Why do programmers prefer dark mode? Because light attracts bugs." I snickered. Yeah.

"Hello, Jeff Davis," Garth said.

"Hi."

"Hey, Jeff!" greeted Scott Stark, my best friend, if you don't count Cheryl. He was kind of my opposite. He seemed to actually enjoy people, and get along with everyone he met.

"Hi, Scott," I replied.

"Good morning, Jeff." That was Doug Grimm. He must have been at least twenty years older than me. I was twenty-eight, so he was pushing fifty. He was nice enough, I guess. He once gave me a gun to protect myself. I'm not sure that was a good idea, because I ended up shooting at my own dad, and intimidating other people with it. That was a dark period of time in my life, but I'm doing a lot better now. It's amazing how much better your life goes when you finally surrender your life to God. Anyway, I threw that gun in the Red River that day when the police were chasing me.

"Hi Doug." I sat down, and went right to my email.

Then, in the midst of our clatter of typing, Garth spat out, "Scott, for the sake of everything holy, you aren't going to type in those blues all day, are you?"

Scott grinned like he was guilty, and not ashamed of it. "I was thinking of it."

I looked around, wondering what "blues" he was referring

to. Not his clothes. He had a different keyboard, but the keys were clearly black, not blue.

"There should be a law against it," Garth continued. "Or at least an office policy."

"I kinda like it. It feels like gaming at work. It lightens the mood."

"It does no such thing. You're annoying everyone around you."

I looked at Doug, and shrugged.

Doug said, "I believe Garth is referring to Scott's mechanical keyboard switches."

I looked at his keyboard again, but his keys were still black.

"His switches," said Garth, "connect his key caps to his mechanical keyboard, and dictate the feel and sound. Scott here is using blue switches, which are the loudest available on the market."

"They're great for gaming," Scott said.

"But not for working in a group setting. Use something else." Garth pointed. "There. That's your usual keyboard. Use that one."

"Fine," said Scott swapping keyboards, "but I won't like it as much. I won't be as happy."

"You can buy yourself some browns, and keep the rest of us happy."

Doug leaned toward me, and commented, "Brown switches are known to be quieter."

We worked in relative quiet for a while, before Garth again broke the silence. "Scott!" he said, leaning in to look closer at his screen. "Did you really name this variable 'first_name'?"

"Oh, probably," Scott replied. "I don't remember every single variable I've ever declared, but if it refers to someone's first name, that sounds like something I'd do. Why? What's wrong with it?"

"Shall I list all the problems with it?"

"Sure. Go for it, Garth. Knock yourself out."

"First of all, the case is wrong. It's in snake case, but should be in camel case."

"Fine. Change it."

"And second, the name of the variable should match the name of the database column, which is 'name_first', not 'first_name.' Therefore, your variable should be 'nameFirst', not 'firstName'."

"That sounds awfully silly," Scott rolled his eyes. "'firstName' is obviously the best name for the variable, since that's what it describes."

Both Garth and Scott swiveled their chairs around so they could face each other. Garth frowned, and began, "Must I explain to you the ways of the programmer?"

"You're free to share your opinion, but I might not take it."

"Yes, it is my opinion, but it is also the correct way to do things. You first establish the category, then you describe the details of that category. For example, consider these attributes: 'address_line_1', 'address_city', 'address_province', 'address_country'. Notice the category first, then the detail?"

Scott rolled his eyes again. "Yeah?"

"It's the same with name: 'name_first', 'name_last', 'name_middle', 'name_salutation', 'name_suffix'. Your variable should be called 'nameFirst', not 'firstName'."

"'firstName' sounds better."

"Programming is not about sound. It is about a systematic assemblage of characters."

"It flows off the tongue better."

"Programming is not spoken with the tongue. It is typed with the fingers."

"It's better English."

"This is not English!"

Just then our boss, Nigel, appeared at the doorway.

"Speaking of an assemblage of characters, our morning meeting is about to begin in the board room."

I was looking forward to this meeting, because if all went well, we might roll out a new version of our software, Omniscient, that we have been working on for a while.

CHAPTER 2

8:03 AM

We developers, as well as some other people, sat around the boardroom table.

Nigel stood, and spoke. "You all have been working very hard the last number of months getting ready for Omniscient version 2.0. Ronja has been working hard to install the beta on our servers, and I'm happy to announce that as of right now, it is available for us to start beta testing in real life. In fact, why don't we get going on it right now?"

We all pulled out our phones and started doing stuff. I was familiar enough with the new version, since I worked on some of it, but it was still fun to poke into all the different parts for real. The biggest new feature was the ability to be more social. Yes, Omniscient was not just the all-singing, all-dancing, communications app that we all knew and loved. Now, it had become social. You could befriend people, and post content to rooms, and hit the like buttons, and all things that made the users of our software more connected. Omniscient was becoming social.

I soon got a friend request from Scott. I accepted it, and friend-requested him back, which he accepted. Yay! Notification sounds of all kinds were flying all over the room.

"Hey look! The programmers are socializing!"

Our four heads lifted up to see who said that. It was Andy,

the sound and graphics guy. It was his sounds that were no doubt playing a symphony in his ears. His pale, leafy green button shirt had huge cuffs and collars. I've always wondered how he could dress so weirdly. I glanced at the four of us programmers. We wore normal clothing, appropriate to an office setting. Well, Garth wore an old Star Wars tee shirt and jeans, but the rest of us looked normal.

"The first thing we should do is test the system." This was Ronja speaking. She was the system administrator, and also in charge of deployment. "I have sent a friend request to Garth. Garth, can you accept it please, to verify everything is working correct?"

Garth rolled his eyes. To my shock, he said, "Oh, all right. If I must." He tapped the button.

Ronja smiled. "Good. It's working. Carry on, everyone."

I got a notification. Someone had invited me to an Omniscient Technologies Developers room. I accepted, and saw that Andy had posted a picture. It was a shot of our four heads looking down.

"Ha, ha," commented Scott, dryly.

"Does a picture of professionals working hard amuse you, Mr. Artist?"

Andy shrugged. "I find amusement where I can get it."

"So, everyone, thank you for working very hard on these new features," Nigel continued. "We have also been working hard on securing our data. All communications to our servers are encrypted, and we are now storing our data encrypted, too, just to make sure." He paused, then asked, "What's the name of our encryption algorithm again?"

"TK15," said Garth. "After much research, this was the best one available that meets all our criteria."

"And it's good for PR," continued Nigel. "We can tell the news and everyone that our data is completely safe in every way. At least I think it is. There are a lot of moving parts here.

Let's go through them all. First of all, communication from the client app to our server."

"The easiest one," said Garth. "That is secure with the highest grade certificate we can get."

"OK, good. What about on our servers?"

"Yes, again."

"What about on the client? What if someone loses their phone?"

"We encrypt data locally, too."

"Good. Anywhere else?"

I spoke up. "Email communication to our server is encrypted, too."

"Good. Anything else?"

Doug posed a question. "What about our database backups?"

Good question. We all looked at each other, then settled on Ronja, because that was her job.

"We do database dumps nightly, which get put into a tarball file, which is then sent securely to our backup service. Our backup service prides itself on being very secure."

"But is the tarball file itself encrypted?"

Ronja hesitated. "It might not be."

Nigel scratched the back of his head. "I'm sure that will be fine," then paused. "But still, can we encrypt them, too?"

"I'm sure we can, somehow."

"You know, I have a great deal of faith in all of you, but I wonder if small things like this can fall between the cracks. Maybe we should hire a security professional to look over everything, and see if there is anything we missed."

Scott shrugged, and said, "Sure."

Garth scowled. "I guess so, if he doesn't force us to partake in any silliness."

"He would just give us advice. We wouldn't have to do anything we don't want to."

"Very well."

"Any other comments? No? OK, then I'll start looking for one. Unless anyone here knows of a security specialist?"

After a pause, I slowly raised my hand. "It seems I have one for a neighbor."

8:55 AM

"Thanks for giving me a ride to the police station, Scott," I said.

"No problem. Any time."

We cruised along in Scott's Mustang.

"Hey, do you think the guy who blew up your car is connected to your dad?"

I shrugged. "Maybe. Maybe I should talk to him about it."

Scott grinned. "You'd talk to your dad? The guy who tried to kill you?"

"Well, he is in jail. He can't hurt me now. And besides, he seems like a much better guy now. He says he's a Christian."

"Seriously! The guy gets Jesus in jail? Wow. Not what I would have expected. Do you believe him?"

"Yeah, I think so." I didn't mention that jail was also where I found Jesus. Well, in a holding cell at a police station anyway, not real jail. And speaking of being locked up, I wasn't looking forward to going back to the police. The last time I was here was because I got arrested.

"You could have gone here by yourself," said Scott.

"I don't have a car, remember?"

"Oh yeah, I forgot."

The police station was in a strip mall. We parked, then walked inside. Past the heavy front door, we were greeted by an officer behind glass. He asked us how he could help, and I told him that my car got blown up the evening before. It didn't surprise him. I suppose news like that carries quickly in the law enforcement circles. He started handing me a clipboard to fill out when he caught himself. "Come to think of it, the officer you will be dealing with specifically requested to talk to you himself." He drew the clipboard back.

I got nervous. Someone wanted to talk with me? This can't be good. I didn't want to be locked up again. But it wasn't my fault. I didn't do anything this time.

"Here he comes now." We heard a loud buzzing and Scott had the presence of mind to open the next door, and walk inside while the unlock buzzer sounded. I followed him.

We were met by a large man with tattoos on his arms. I didn't remember seeing them before, but maybe I just never saw this man in short sleeves.

"If it isn't Jeff Davis and Scott Stark!" he said to us. "Something told me you two might be involved in this."

"Hi, Detective," I said.

"Hey, Joseph!," said Scott. The detective scowled. "It's Detective Wakefield to you. You two may as well come with me.

We followed him to his office. It was the same one with the wooden chair that squeaked.

"I thought you dealt with cybercrime," I said.

"I quit. Couldn't take it. I'm back on murder. Cybercrime is too new. Murder is old. Old as the hills. People have been killing each other since Cain and Abel." He drilled his eyes into mine, forcing me to confess to something I'd either done or once thought about doing. I didn't dare admit I'd heard of the story of Cain and Abel, or he might accuse me of being an accomplice. I sat still and said nothing.

"Nobody died," added Scott, almost cheerfully.

"It was attempted murder," growled Joseph. "Close enough in my book. Now tell me everything." He took out a notepad and started writing.

We told him everything we knew, which was almost

nothing.

"I'm going to track down security camera footage of that parking lot. The bomb itself was probably your standard fair, remotely detonated. Frankly, I'm surprised you survived."

I was shocked. "Why?"

"Because if it was remotely detonated, why did the perpetrator trigger it too soon? Why not wait until you were in the car?"

I didn't know. I had nothing to say.

"Maybe someone wasn't trying to kill Jeff?" Scott asked.

"Maybe someone is trying to shake you up. Get your attention. I'd watch my back if I was you."

I slouched back in my chair. Great. Again with the worrying. Maybe I should get a gun again. No, that didn't go so well last time.

He continued. "It might not be a remote control next time. It might be activated by you opening the door or stepping on the gas or brake pedal. It could be anything."

My eyes were wide, and I was trying to control my breathing.

"You're scaring him, Joseph," said Scott.

The detective scowled at Scott, then said, "He's in danger for his life. If he's careful, he might live through it."

"Of course he will," said Scott.

"Yeah. Hopefully, anyway. Now, Jeff," He leaned back and his wooden chair squeaked. "Tell me who you ticked off this time so bad he wants to kill ya."

"Nobody," I replied.

"Really?! It was just a coincidence that the guy who keeps putting the bad guys in jail gets his car blown up?"

I shrugged. "All the bad guys I know are already in jail."

"Then it was probably one of them, or a buddy of his. They can call in a hit from jail, you know."

"It probably wasn't my dad."

"You mean Jade? Why not?"

I shrugged again. "He seems to be a better person now. He says he became a Christian."

"I've met a few people claiming to be followers of Jesus. I've arrested some, and convicted some of them."

This time I scowled. "Really?"

"Yeah. You think being a Christian makes you perfect? It doesn't, apparently."

"It should."

"Welcome to the real world, my friend. Some people are bad people, even some who say they're Christians. And they might be, I can't say. Jade might be one of them."

I shook my head. "No."

"Suit yourself. What about his buddy there, what's his name? Max?"

"Max never did like me."

The policeman rubbed the back of his head. "I remember that guy. I didn't like him, either. I still don't. But he's still sitting in jail. Then there's that other gang, led by Yash Nagi. He's in jail. So are his henchmen, including the one who murdered your boss. They're all in jail, but they all could still be coming after you."

It was all true. I sat there, not knowing who was after me, and not knowing what I should do, or could do. I'm glad Scott was here. It's easier with someone with you.

"Don't worry, Jeff," said Scott. "We made it through other stuff. We'll make it through this, too."

"Thanks."

"If I discover anything, I'll let you know," said Joseph. "Your email address is still the same?"

"Yes."

Scott grinned, "But he keeps breaking his phone."

I rolled my eyes. "It's not me who keeps breaking it."

"Tell you what." Scott reached into his pocket and took out

his smartphone. "You can have mine."

"What? You're giving me your phone?"

"Sure. I need a new one anyway, and you could use a backup."

"Are you sure?"

"Yeah. You're my friend, and it gives me a good excuse to buy a new one."

"Um... thanks, Scott." I slipped it into a pocket on my cargo pants.

"Do a factory reset on it."

"I sure will." I didn't know what might be lingering on his phone, and I didn't want to find out.

The detective added, "And if you find out anything, send it to me."

"OK," I replied. "But maybe you should increase your maximum attachment size. I tried sending you a video, and it didn't work, remember?"

"Yeah. Maybe we should look into that."

He lifted up his hands, then set them down again. I didn't know what that meant, but maybe it was that our meeting was over. I stood. So did Scott. "Thanks, Detective."

He stayed put. "Stay safe, Jeff."

On our way out of the building, Scott said to me, "I've suddenly got a hankering for an Ice Cap. You want to get an Ice Cap with me?"

"I'd love to."

9:59 AM

As Scott and I stood in line at Tim Horton's, waiting to order our Iced Cappuccinos, my mind started to wander. I thought about our new version of Omniscient, and how we can mark each other as friends. If a group was the same size as this restaurant, say... twenty people in here, the number of different combinations of friends would be twenty people squared. People got up and sat down around me. No, make that twenty times nineteen, because you can't friend yourself. That's not a big number for a computer. But what about an organization of two thousand people? That could be large. That's why you add an index to your database table. As these thoughts were buzzing around my head, another part of my head tried to get my attention. But I wasn't listening, because I was busy analyzing this algorithm. And hopefully we never have to go through that whole list, because that's an expensive operation, like a big oh of n squared. My other brain shouted even louder, until finally I woke up and started listening. It screamed at me, "Look! We know that man!"

I turned my head toward where my brain was pointing. Subconsciously, I had watched a man walk out of the washroom, through the cafe, and out the doors. For some reason, after he was outside, he looked in, and our eyes locked. Then he started running.

I smacked Scott on the back and almost shouted, "Scott! That man may have done it!"

He turned, and, looking out the last window, he saw the man running. Without saying a word, he bolted for the door. I followed.

We glanced around, but saw no one. Then we ran to the side of the building, hoping he might still be there. He was, getting into his car. It was a gray Honda Civic, like my old one. By the time we were there, he was already backing out. Scott pounded on the driver's side window commanding him to open the door. I yelled, "We just want to talk!"

I could see the man looked nervous. He just wanted to get away. I ran around, and stood behind the vehicle, hoping he would not want to run me over. He just backed up slowly enough that I wouldn't get hurt. When he was clear of all the cars, I knew he was going to take off fast, so without thinking, I jumped onto the back bumper and held on to some small gap between body panels. It might not have been a very smart thing to do, but I was desperate. I made it all the way to the end of the parking lot before I couldn't take it anymore, and had to jump off.

I stood there, staring at the receding tail lights, distraught that I wouldn't be able to talk to this man, wondering if he was even involved, but if he wasn't then why was he running away? Then another car pulled up beside me and honked. It was a Mustang, Scott's Mustang. I got in, and suddenly there was a chance I'd still get some answers today.

We didn't talk much during the chase. At first, Scott said something about us catching up to him fast since he was only in a Civic, and we were in a real car, but after a few minutes of weaving through traffic, and not getting much closer, he didn't make that comment again. That's one point for us Civic drivers, I guess.

He led us South on Pembina. At first, I thought he might be trying to get to the highway, but then realized that that would be good, because then our car could really take him. As it was, he was smaller, and more agile. He could dodge and weave, and he was doing an excellent job at it.

"You know, this cherry red doesn't help us blend in very well," I said.

"Who wants to blend in? Life is about being seen." I shook my head. Scott and I were not the same person.

"He turned off!" I shouted.

"I see him!"

He suddenly took a left, straight through an intersection, on a red light. Then he continued in a U-turn to come back the same way.

It looked like Scott considered driving over the median, but he knew better. Instead, he headed right into the intersection, in front of blaring horns and swerving cars. I closed my eyes hoping we wouldn't get hit. By some miracle we didn't. Then Scott floored the gas, because our lane was now empty, but once we got up to speed, the man's car was gone.

We looked around frantically, hoping he pulled off to one side.

"I see him!" I yelled and pointed out my window. There, in the parking lot of a big box store was the little gray Civic. He was still driving fast. Scott hammered the brakes, spun the car around to find the entrance, then rocketed toward the large building.

"We could go right," I suggested, because the man we were chasing had turned right on the far end of the building, to go around it to the right. If we went right now, around the building on this side, we might meet him at the back. Scott cranked the wheel to the right.

"Agh!" Scott moaned, because there was a minivan turning left, to go around the back, right where we wanted to, and it was traveling awfully slowly. Scott leaned on the horn, and started to go around him, but this only caused the driver to look around for us, and thus not in front of him, and since he wasn't looking, he drove headlong into a vehicle coming very quickly from around the corner. He hit the gray Civic, and the resultant collision almost hit us. Scott leaned the wheel to the right to avoid it, causing his car to slide sideways along the pavement, then hit a curb at an angle which spun us around even more. When we came to a stop, I was breathing heavily, and clutching whatever I could find to steady myself.

Scott, however, was already out of the car, sprinting toward the other accident.

The man I had seen at the coffee shop was staggering out of his car, but when he saw Scott barreling toward him, he turned and tried running away. He only got as far as a patch of grass when Scott's full weight came bearing down on him, toppling them both to the ground.

I ran out to join them. Now, we were going to get some answers.

CHAPTER 3

10:31 AM

"Get off me!" he yelled.

"No," Scott replied. "Tell me who you are."

"Get off me!"

"Who are you?"

"I'm nobody!"

"Then why were you running from us?"

The man only struggled more.

"If you're nobody," Scott repeated, "why were you running? You could have killed yourself with that driving of yours."

"I was running for my life."

"From who?"

"Who?! From you!"

Scott looked confused, and looked up at me. "Do you know this guy?"

"Yeah."

"Who is he?"

"He's Yash Nagi's butler."

"Is this true?" Scott demanded of the man.

"I was. Until he went to jail. Now I'm unemployed."

"Why do you think we would kill you?"

"Why?! Because my boss tried to kill you, or rather Jeff Davis here. Listen. Can I get up, please? You're on my back."

"Promise you won't run?"

"Promise you won't hurt me?"

"Promise," said Scott, then he got up and let the man roll over onto his back, and sit up. "What's your name?" he asked the man.

"James Kuff. Who are you?"

"I'm Jeff's friend Scott. And if you tried to kill my friend, I'm no friend of yours."

"I did no such thing. I was only employed as a butler. That's it. I never got involved in anything shady."

"But you didn't try to stop them either."

"They had guns!"

Now I asked a question. "Did you blow up my car?"

He stared up at me. "What? No!" Then reality dawned on him. "Oh, that was your car!" He held up his hands. "I had nothing to do with that. I'm just a simple man looking for work."

"What kind of work are you looking for?"

He scowled at me as if I were stupid. "Being a butler, preferably."

"He's unemployed, remember?" Scott reminded me.

"Oh. Right." Then back to James, I said, "You might still have connections. Have you heard anything about the car bomb?"

The man shook his head "No. I'm out of the loop. I have no idea what's going on."

I looked around, wondering what to do now, then back at the man. "If you hear anything, will you let us know?"

He chuckled. "Why should I?"

"It's the right thing to do."

"You're funny, Jeff. 'The right thing to do.'"

Just then another man came up from behind us. "Hey, is everyone all right here?" We turned. It must have been the minivan driver.

"Yup," I said.

"Yeah," said Scott.

James got up. "Good enough."

Scott said to me, "Let's take off. These guys can sort themselves out."

We walked back to the car.

"You are OK, aren't you?" Scott asked me.

"I'm fine. You?"

"Yeah, I'm good. I hope my car's OK."

We examined it, and with the exception of a few scuffs on the tires, it seemed to be fine. That was a relief. Just then my phone buzzed at me. It was a message from Cheryl. It said, "I need to talk with you."

11:05 AM

"I had a dream about you." Cheryl accosted me as I walked up the stairs leading to the Johnston Terminal where we worked. Scot had dropped me off, and was out parking his car.

I smiled back at Cheryl. "I dream about you all the time, Cheryl."

She didn't smile back. Instead, she sat down on the steps, so I sat down next to her, and placed my hand on her knee. "What did you dream?"

She looked up and sighed. "I dreamed you were walking down a road, toward a light, and people like you were following you."

"People like me?"

"Yes. You know, they were like you, but not you. Just like you."

"OK."

"And you were magnetized, and other people appeared and were drawn to you."

I squinted in thought, trying to understand this. "OK..."

"And one of them was a woman."

"Was it you?" I asked hopefully.

"No! It was a woman with long dark hair. And she was attracted to you, Jeff. And you were embracing her." She grabbed a lock of her short red hair, and asked, "Does this look like long black hair to you?"

It was a trap. There was no way out of this situation. I couldn't lie, and I couldn't just not answer, so I said, "No."

"Then who is the woman with long black hair?"

"I don't know! I'm not attracted to anyone but you, Cheryl."

"You were in the dream."

"It's just a dream. It doesn't mean anything."

She took a deep breath, and tried to let it out slowly. "I think it does. I've had dreams before, dreams that were from God. Dreams mean things, Jeff."

"What do you think this means? It can't mean that I'm attracted to someone else."

"Well, the first part is obvious."

"What? What's obvious?"

"The people following you, who were like you, are obviously the other developers."

I laughed. "They're certainly not following me."

"They will. You're walking toward the light, remember? The light is God, and you are leading the others toward God."

That one hit close to home. Months ago, God told me to share his email address with the other developers, and what did I do? Nothing. I'm supposed to be leading them toward God, and what have I done to that end? Not a thing. I haven't mentioned it to them even once. I even tried hosting a pizza party with the sole intention of telling them his email address then, but I chickened out, just like every time before, just like I always do. I was beginning to think it would never happen. However, this dream of Cheryl's almost gives me hope. If she dreamed that I did it, maybe I could do it. Maybe I should do it right now. I started to take out my phone to compose an email, but Cheryl interrupted.

"But then who's the dark-haired woman?"

I shook my head. "I have no idea. Maybe a family member."

"Do you have any sisters?"

"One, but she lives in Texas."

"What's her hair color?"

"Short and brown, like me."

"What about your mother?"

"Also brown. And curly."

She leaned toward me and pointed her large eyes straight at mine. "Promise me you're not now, nor will you ever start seeing a long, dark-haired woman."

I couldn't help but smile at her concern. Truth be told, it felt good to be wanted, and I had no intention of going to anyone else. "I promise. I promise I am not now, nor will I ever start seeing a long, dark-haired woman."

With those words, her shoulders relaxed, and so did her tight expression. Then she wrapped her arms around my chest and said, "Good."

I instinctively put my arms around her too. "I love you, Cheryl. I only ever want to see more of you. That's it."

"Thanks. I know. It just feels good to hear it."

We stood up. As she leaned in to give me a kiss, I had a flashback to another point in time, many months ago when another woman at this very spot tried to lean in to give me a kiss. Suddenly I knew who the dark-haired woman was.

We walked back into the building in silence, holding hands.

12:00 Noon

As I sat at my desk, working, my phone chirped. I didn't recognize this particular chirp, so I looked at it. Oh, right. It's our new version of Omniscient. I went to the settings and tried other sounds. There was a bling, a blong, a woo-woo, and a chazee. I didn't like any of them. I thought the shushushang might sound better, but everything was either too loud, too quiet, obnoxious, or silly. Just to be sure, I listened to the bang-footh, the chirchirkow, and the hows-hows-i. I finally settled on the twiggersnakle.

"Are you done?" Scott asked, tired of my noise-making.

"Yeah," I replied. "Who came up with these, anyway?"

"Andy, I guess."

"I sometimes think he has too much time on his hands."

Then I remembered to check what the actual notification was for. It was from our boss Nigel. It read, "As appreciation for many months of hard work on Omniscient version 3, pizza is served in the staff kitchen. You are all welcome."

"Hey! Pizza!" I stood up and put my phone in my pocket, just as it twigglesnakled at me. I took it out again. Garth replied to Nigel with, "And drinks?" I glanced up at Garth who sat hunched at his desk, apparently working, except for the Omniscient window open on his screen.

Soon Nigel replied, "There is always Dr. Pepper for you, Garth. I made sure of it personally."

At this, Garth stood up. "There are worse bosses to work for."

We made our way to the kitchen where we found boxes of pizza arrayed on the central table. If there had been cheese, I would have taken that. Instead, I took a piece of pepperoni and a bottle of water and sat down next to Cheryl, who was seated next to her boss, Kaleisha, the head of customer service.

Garth took two pieces of fully-loaded and the large bottle of Dr. Pepper, and also found a seat.

Nigel was already there, and once we had settled down, he got our attention, and started making a speech. "First of all, I would like to thank all the developers for making an outstanding product!" He clapped, and everyone else did too. "If it wasn't for you, the rest of us wouldn't be here. Customer service, you do a great job keeping everyone happy." More clapping. "And everyone else from marketing to accounting, you keep the organization running smoothly. Thank you everyone!"

As he sat down, Kaleisha added, "And thanks to Nigel too, a great VP of technology!"

We clapped, and then settled down to talk among ourselves. Garth, a little late, raised the bottle of Dr. Pepper and said, "The best boss a man could have."

Kaleisha added, "Or woman."

I expected that conversation to be over, but Garth continued it. "I was using the term 'man' gender-inclusively."

At that I expected the conversation to be over again, but Kaleisha decided to keep it going. "'Man' is not a gender-inclusive word. It refers to males."

Garth snickered. "You've heard the phrase, 'No man is an island'? Are you suggesting women are islands? Or what about the great Shakespeare who said, 'This above all: to thine own self be true, And it must follow, as the night the day, Thou canst not then be false to any man.' Are you suggesting thou can be false to a woman?"

Suddenly things became a little too awkward for me. This conversation was turning to confrontation. I looked for a place to hide. Maybe I should go for more drinks or pizza, but I still had plenty in front of me. Maybe I should go back to work. No, that would be even more awkward.

Kaleisha may have been the one person in the building who could stand up to Garth. She said, "That was hundreds of years ago, honey. Things change."

"So you admit that 'man' was once gender inclusive?"

"That was a long time ago."

"In 1955, Erich Fromm said, 'In the nineteenth century the problem was that God is dead; in the twentieth century the problem is that man is dead.' Now my question to you, Kaleisha Knowles, is this. Do you truly think anyone in 1955 sincerely thought Erich Fromm was only referring to males? Or was he using the term gender inclusively?"

Kaleisha stared at the man for a second, then conceded, "Fine. He probably thought he was being inclusive."

"And his audience thought it to?"

"Sure. Fine. Them too. So what? It's still sexist. Things change."

I sat quietly and slowly chewed my pizza. Maybe I should try to change the subject. No, that wouldn't work. These two were like King Kong and Godzilla, fighting it out. I'd be lucky to not get taken out in the process.

Garth sounded like he was only getting warmed up. "My point is that using the male pronouns, 'he', 'him', 'man', 'men', is not only not sexist, but it is anti-sexist. It is not lifting up males to a place of prominence, but actually lowering us down to a place of humility."

I almost choked. What? Humility? What does Garth know about humility? He's the most arrogant man, I mean person, I know.

"Garth! You're crazy!" Kaleisha shook her head. I thought she was going to get up and walk out, leaving Garth the clear winner. Maybe sheer curiosity at this astounding statement kept her in her seat. "H.. ho... how can you say that?!"

Garth leaned back, took a bite of pizza, and proceeded to lecture us with a full mouth. "You see," he began, if 'he' refers to either gender, and 'she' refers only to females, then females have their own pronoun, don't they? And males don't. And since we don't have a word to refer to our own gender, and you do, clearly you are at an advantage, and we are at a disadvantage. And therefore, using "he" and "man" gender-inclusively is one of the most valuable and self-sacrificial gifts a man can give a woman." He continued to chew.

The whole room was silent. Even Kaleisha sat there, mouth open, with no words coming out. Before she was able to form any syllables, Garth finished her off. "You are speechless, I see," he said. "I get that a lot. But don't feel too bad. Not many can match wits with me. You did pretty good, all things considered. This is good pizza. Nigel, where does this come from?"

I think Nigel was also eager to change the subject, because he answered "Za Pizza," then went on to talk about the sale they were having and how they made each custom pizza from scratch right in front of you. By the time he was done, the tension in the room had cooled off a little. Kaleisha had gone to sit somewhere else. I started breathing easier.

Garth himself was probably the biggest reason I hadn't shared God's email address with him yet. I just couldn't imagine his response. And whatever I did imagine, it didn't end well.

CHAPTER 4

1:09 PM

In programming, unlike in math, variables are not just numbers. They can also be words, known as strings, or they can be integers, without any decimal places, or floating point numbers, which are numbers with decimals and an exponent. Another type is called boolean, which can hold only one of two values: True or False.

I sat there, programming the next feature of Omniscient, working with a boolean variable, true or false, when a small thought popped into my head. It said, "I Am the Truth." Before I got to know this God of mine a while ago, I would have dismissed such a thought as a random stray and wouldn't have given it a second chance. Now, however, I suspected it came from God. In fact, I recognized it as such.

I whispered back, "Hello, Truth."

He said, "Hi, Jeff," with a smile and a wink. I didn't hear or see this remark, I just felt it. I just felt the thought land on my mind.

I continued programming.

A few minutes later, my thoughts began to wander again. I thought about my dad's car, I mean my car, exploding. I thought about Cheryl calling me at home. I thought about my mom calling me at home. She had said, "Jeff, tell me that wasn't your car." I had said, "Of course not." I was saving her undo stress and worry. I was protecting her.

I continued working, but I began to see errors show up in my console. Something wasn't working. I was obviously messing up somehow. "Tell me that wasn't your car." "Of course not." I was getting frustrated, and I couldn't figure out what I was doing wrong. I scowled. Time for coffee.

My cup was empty, so I retreated to the kitchen for more, but of course the pot was empty, so I started making more. After I grabbed a packet of coffee grounds from the drawer, in my frustration I must have slammed the drawer shut a little too fast and loud, because Cheryl walked in and noticed. "What's wrong?" she asked.

I looked up. "Nothing."

"Really?"

"I was getting errors, and I don't know what I was doing wrong."

"That makes you this upset? I thought you enjoyed the challenge."

I threw up my hands. "Then I don't know."

She came and held my hands, and looked up into my eyes. "There must be something going on inside your heart."

I looked back into her eyes, lost in her beauty, and smiled. "I always feel better when I'm with you."

She let go of my hands. "Maybe you shouldn't."

"What? What?" I was confused.

"Maybe you shouldn't feel better. Maybe you should confront these feelings."

Here we go with feelings. What was it with women and feelings? I'm just trying to program a computer. She continued. "Maybe instead of running away, you should confront these feelings. Now, what were you just doing or thinking about?"

Fine, for Cheryl, I'll talk about my feelings. "I was working."

"What were you thinking about?"

"I was thinking about... when my mom called me yesterday."

"And what did she say, or what did you say?"

"She asked if the car that blew up was mine. I said no."

"But it was your car."

"I was protecting her."

She angled her head. "Is that what you call it?"

"I was. Why? What would you call it?"

"It doesn't matter what I call it. What would God say?"

"I'm a little frustrated. I don't feel like listening right now."

She sat at a table, and patted the seat next to her. "Come sit with me," she smiled.

I couldn't resist her, so I sat.

"Now close your eyes."

I closed them.

"Now let's ask the Lord. God, why is Jeff feeling upset?"

I opened an eye and peaked at her.

"No peeking! Listen. What comes to your mind?"

I smirked and said, "God says I would feel better if you kissed me." Then I laughed out loud.

"Jeff! This is important!"

"OK, fine." I relaxed and imagined God standing next to me. Then I remembered the thought that came to me a few minutes ago. I Am the Truth. I opened my eyes. "He says, 'I Am the Truth.'".

"Very good. And were you speaking the truth when you lied to your mom?"

I looked up and sideways, and finally shrugged. "I... I was trying to protect her."

"OK, we'll ask God again. Close your eyes. God, please show Jeff what it's like to lie to his mom. Is he really protecting her?"

I closed my eyes, and tried to listen or look or be sensitive to whatever might come to me. I said, "A picture comes to my mind of my mom tied to a chair with a belt."

"A belt?"

"Yes. That's what came to mind. You asked what came to my mind, and it was a belt."

"OK. Do you know what it means?"

"No. Do you?"

"I have a pretty good idea, but you need to hear from God yourself. God, what does this mean? Can you please explain it to us?"

This time I didn't even need to close my eyes. Suddenly it became clear. I sighed again. "The belt that my mom was tied up with is a lie. If you speak the truth, it's like a belt that holds your pants up, but if you lie, you are tying other people up... not protecting them." Suddenly I felt even worse. I scowled and got up to check the coffee. It wasn't done yet.

"Jeff, you're not done yet," Cheryl said as she walked up to me. She poked her finger onto my chest and said these words. "God has put his spirit inside of you. And when you do things, or say things, or think things that don't line up with his perfect ways, his spirit will try to correct you. He will try to steer you out of the ditch you just drove into. And the reason you are feeling frustrated is because you know what you did was wrong."

I looked back at her. "OK. Fine. Now what?"

She smiled up at me. "Now, you need to get out of the ditch and back onto the road."

"How do you recommend I do that?"

"This is the easy part. You say sorry to God for lying, and try not to lie anymore."

"That's it?"

"Well, maybe more, but it's a great start."

"Fine." I looked off to the side and said, "God, I'm sorry for lying to my mom." Suddenly with those words spoken, I felt a heavy burden lift off of me. I felt almost like laughing and crying, but not quite. "Wow. That does feel better."

"Good for you, Jeff. Now you should call your mom, too."

I was about to object strongly, but realized she was completely right.

I took out my phone, but before I could dial, my boss Nigel appeared and said, "Jeff, thanks for the tip this morning." I was about to ask what he was talking about, but he continued. "I hired the security expert you recommended."

Then Larry also appeared and waved. "Hi Jeff!" he said.

1:31 PM

"Ronja is out buying a graphics card," Nigel said, "so Jeff, can you show Larry around?"

"Sure." I didn't want to, of course. I don't really like people on a good day, and there was something about this guy that I don't like either. He just seems a bit weird.

Nigel said, "Thanks!" and left.

"So, Jeff, where should we start?" Larry asked.

"Uh... the server room, I guess." We took a few steps down the hall, I unlocked the server room, and we went in. I pointed at various things around the room. "This is where the Internet comes in. This is the demilitarized zone, and this is the local network."

"Do you have a Wi-Fi access point?"

"Yes."

"Is it on its own network?"

"Um... I don't think so."

"It should be."

"Why?

"Because anyone from the general public can try to hack your Wi-Fi, and if they succeed, they have instant access to your local network."

"I guess that makes sense."

"You need to section off your networks."

"OK."

"Different networks for different things."

"OK."

"One for developers, one for accountants, one for network printers, that sort of thing."

"Why?"

"Different networks can do different things. The public Wi-Fi can't do much, but you developers can do more. Local devices can reach into the printer network to print something, but no printer should be able to access your desktop, just in case one gets hacked. And nobody can reach the accountants' network."

I frowned. "I'm not sure I like this idea."

"Why not?"

"It impedes what I can do."

"Nobody needs to do everything."

"So there's no all-powerful network I can be a part of?"

"All-powerful? What, you want something like god-mode on a network? That's cheating. No, there is no God network. And if there was, I'd take it down."

"Why?"

"Too powerful. Your people need to be reigned in so they don't do anything dumb. It's for their own good. People aren't that smart." He leaned in to me and lowered his voice. "People are basically morons. If you give them their freedom, you're making a mistake."

"Maybe they need to be set free so they can do more stuff."

"That might be, but if they click a bad link and get a virus, it's your fault." He pointed his finger at me as if I were the system administrator, which I was not. "It's either you or them, right?" He snickered. I didn't answer right away, so he pressed his point. "If something goes wrong, someone's going to take the blame, and you sure don't want it to be you, right? You gotta look out for number one, right?" He stood there, waiting for me to answer, as if he actually cared that I did.

I finally said, "I guess so."

He smiled again. "That's right, Jeff. You look out for number one. Because if you don't, that's when you get hurt."

I didn't like the way he said that last word. It didn't sound very friendly.

After a brief moment of awkwardness, at least on my part, he said, "Well, let's start by setting up some VLANs."

I said, "VLAN?"

"Virtual LAN, virtual local area network. You can change all the networks in software, not hardware. And we'll get rid of your all-powerful network."

I was about to tell him that I didn't have access to any of the routers or switches, so I couldn't actually help him, when Ronja walked in holding a brand new graphics card in a box, and said, "What is going on?"

I explained to her that Larry was hired to do a security assessment or something like that, and needed access to stuff that I couldn't help him with. Then I made my way to the door.

On my way out, Larry said, "I'll talk to you later, Jeff!"

"OK," I replied over my shoulder.

1:58 PM

The coffee I had consumed finished making its way through the network called my body, and when I had taken care of that, I came back to my desk to find an envelope with "For Jeff Davis" written on it. "What's this?" I asked out loud.

"Larry put it there," said Scott. "He said he found it on the ground outside."

I opened the envelope and started reading. Suddenly everything changed. My heart beat faster, and I started to sweat. My hands may have begun shaking ever so slightly. Scott looked up at me. "What's wrong?" he said.

"I... I have to go." I rushed out and found Larry still in the server room. "Where did you find this?" I asked.

"It was outside the main doors. Why? What is it?"

I didn't answer, but instead went straight to the receptionist. "Did you, by any chance see Larry bring this in here?"

She responded with, "Who's Larry again?"

"The consultant."

"Oh, yes. He picked it up just out there and brought it in. I told him where your desk was."

"Thanks," I replied, not feeling very thankful.

"You're welcome! Why? What is it?"

"I... uh... hopefully nothing." I started toward Cheryl's desk, then changed my mind. I didn't want her to read this. I went the other direction—out the doors and down the stairs. I didn't feel safe in the office. I was halfway down the stairs when I realized I didn't feel safe outside either. I sat down, and put my head in my trembling hands.

I prayed the only thing I could think of. "God, help me!" As soon as I did, I felt a hand on my shoulder. I whipped my head around, expecting to see a gun pointed at my face, held by an evil man grinning wickedly. Instead it was Scott, who sat down beside me, and took the letter out of my hands. "Give this to me," he said, and read it to himself. I didn't want to hear the words spoken out loud, but took some comfort in the fact that I now didn't have to carry the weight of them by myself.

Scott said, "It says, 'Why should I let you live?'" He sighed and glanced around us. Of course there was nobody to see, no masked man hiding around a corner, no mysterious person in a trench coat standing nearby staring at us. There were only regular, normal people, going about their boring lives, not knowing I was going to be murdered.

"Someone's trying to kill me," I managed to say.

"No," my friend simply replied.

"What? How can you say that? I just got a death threat."

"No, if he wanted you dead, you'd be dead already."

I rolled my eyes. "Thanks!"

"It's not a death threat. It's a note saying you are still alive. He's keeping you alive for a reason. As long as that reason stays around, you will stay around."

I was probably supposed to find that thought comforting. I didn't feel very comforted.

"I should go to the police."

"Might not be the best thing to do."

"Why not?"

"Well, you know, you don't want to push this guy too far. You don't want to give him a reason to change his mind."

"And decide to kill me for real?"

He shrugged. "Yup."

I stood up and leaned against the railing. "So you're saying I'm safe?"

"For the moment, yeah, you might be."

"I don't feel very safe." We stood around awkwardly, as if Scott might give me a hug to comfort me, but that would be weird. I might have also taken that hug, to make me feel better, but that still would have been weird. So instead, I said, "I think I'll go for a walk."

"Are you going to be OK?"

I shrugged. "Yeah, I guess. I'll be back." I turned, and made my way toward the river. There was someone there I needed to talk to.

2:17 PM

As I exited the Johnston Terminal, I half expected to see the person who slipped me the note outside waiting for me to explain to me why he was letting me live, and when he was going to kill me. But there was no such person. There were people here and there, but nobody approached me. Nobody even looked at me. I was alone.

I wandered down the concrete steps toward the river, where I walked along a pathway next to it. At one point I sat down on a bench and watched the little waves over the Assiniboine River. The sun was out and there was a small breeze. Some birds splashed in the river. They had no idea what was going on with me. They didn't know my life could end at any moment. The very next car I touched might be my last.

I took out my phone and started taking notes. I wrote my name, a colon, then "God, there is someone trying to kill me," then I closed my eyes, and imagined God sitting next to me on the bench. He was wearing a white robe. The wind slowly tossed his brown hair around. He wasn't looking out at the river like I was. He had his eyes fixed on me, and was smiling with peaceful contentment. Some words came to my mind, so I wrote them down.

"God: Your life is in my hands. Don't worry, child."

That did make me feel a little better. I wrote, "Jeff: Thanks. Does that mean I'm not going to die?"

A thought came to me, so I wrote that down too.

"God: Most people die. Even Jesus died."

"Jeff: I mean soon."

"God: What are you trying to do? Live forever? Is that the goal here?"

"Jeff: Well, it might be nice."

"God: When your time is up and you're standing before me, are you going to get points for a long life? Or will you get rewarded for doing what I have called you to do, in the amount of time I have given you?"

"Jeff: OK, what are you calling me to do?"

"God: Love me and love other people."

"Jeff: And how am I supposed to love other people?"

"God: By giving to them. Give your money. If you're not faithful with your worldly wealth, who will give you true riches? Also, give your life, because there is no greater act of love than to give your life for your friends."

"Jeff: More talk of dying."

"God: If a seed wants to live and produce fruit, it first has to lie down in the ground and essentially die. Jeff, I want you to live. I want you to produce fruit. So start loving people. Start giving."

I looked up and pondered some clouds floating by for a minute, then continued. "Jeff: That sounds backwards to me. The advice I've heard is to pursue your dreams, not run away from them."

"God: If you want to make money in the stock market, or some business venture, what's the first thing you do? You give your money away, and hope it will come back to you multiplied. In the same way, you need to begin by first giving what you have."

I chuckled to myself. Now I was getting investing advice from God. Actually, that might be a great idea. "Jeff: Buy low, sell high, get a piece of the pie? Is that it? Isn't that what everybody does? That doesn't sound backwards to me."

"God: Remember that when prices are low, which is when you should buy, everybody else is selling. And when prices are high, which is when you should sell, everybody else is buying. You can't follow what everybody else is doing. You have to act counter to the culture. Jeff, I'm calling you to stand out. Be different. Play by a different set of rules, my rules. Learn my ways, and don't follow the rest of the world. Be different."

I stood up. Those were crazy words. They would require some thought. This was backwards thinking right here.

I ambled back down the path, with my eyes on the ground,

pondering what was just said. I thought about how I was following the world, and how I should be "counter-cultural". I thought about giving, and what I could give.

When I was almost back to the Johnson Terminal, I finally looked up, and something caught my eye. In the building across from ours, which was mostly a food court, I noticed a new business which was not a food court. It was a bank, a small branch office of the bank where I did my banking. Then I had an idea of something I could do.

CHAPTER 5

4:39 PM

"Ooo! You should use the nullish coalescing operator," said Scott, looking over my shoulder.

"The what?" I replied.

"You've never heard of the nullish coalescing operator?"

"No. Well, maybe."

"It's like the ternary operator," interjected Garth, "but with only two operands."

I scowled, still confused.

"It's the double question mark," said Doug, "instead of just one."

"I've heard of the question mark operator," I said.

"The question mark operator, as you call it, is better known as the ternary operator," said Garth. "And the nullish coalescing operator returns the first operand unless it equates to null, hence the term 'nullish', in which case it returns the second, thus it coalesces."

"And it's cool!" Scott almost shouted. He showed me which parts of my code to change, and remove, and how to use this thing, which I did. It simplified things significantly.

I'm not sure I understood all those fancy terms, but I caught on to the general idea of how to use it. "Wow, nice." I commented.

I added some finishing touches to the code I was writing as

the other guys started packing up for the day. Then Cheryl popped in and said, "Jeff, I can't give you a ride home. My mom is taking me for supper, and dress shopping. Just me and her."

Before I could say a word in response, someone else beat me to it. It wasn't one of us developers. It was the security expert who was also my neighbor. "I'll take Jeff home. He is my neighbor, after all."

I looked to Scott, who said, "Sorry, I've got a date at five. I've gotta run."

Cheryl smiled, "Good! That's taken care of. Have a great evening, Jeff!" And she disappeared around the corner.

Before I knew what was going on, it was somehow assumed I was going home with this guy, Larry, and I couldn't think of a way out of it, so I said, "Um... thanks."

Larry stuck his thumb up, and with a huge grin on his face, said, "It'll be fun!"

I said, "OK."

Pretty soon we were walking out of the building, and toward his car, which was an ancient, light brown Oldsmobile. I wondered how successful this guy could be at being a security specialist if this was the car he was driving. We got in and slammed the doors shut. The car was heavy, but it gave a relaxing ride.

"So, do you have a girlfriend, Jeff?" Larry asked.

"Yeah. Cheryl. She works in customer service."

"Ah, I see. Why?"

"Why what?"

"Why do you have a girlfriend? Doesn't she just slow you down?"

"Slow me down?"

"I'm sure there are things you are trying to do with your life. Having a girlfriend would just get in the way."

"Well..."

"Didn't Jade kidnap your other girlfriend, and force you to come to him?"

I looked at this guy, wondering how he got this information. He just looked back at me, waiting for a reply, so I said, "Well, yes."

"Then why are you putting yourself in that position again?"

"Of having a girlfriend?"

"Yeah"

"Um... well... I guess the real problem is having an evil man out there who is willing to kidnap someone. That's the problem. Not having a girlfriend."

"If there is something you can do to protect yourself, you should do it. There will always be people out there trying to stop your plans. Forming emotional bonds is a risk, because people can take advantage of them. I'm surprised you're letting emotions stand in your way."

This may have been the first time I was ever accused of being emotional, but I was curious to know what he was talking about. "Standing in the way of what, exactly?"

"Aren't you trying to 'clean up this city'? You've already put away Jade, and Yash Nagi, and some of their guys. It seems you're on some sort of crusade."

I shrugged. "Not really."

"Ha! Is that so?"

The real answer is that I just do whatever God tells me to do, but I didn't want to use those words, so I replied, "I just do whatever."

"Regardless, I'm not surprised someone is trying to kill you. You've made some enemies."

Yeah, that part was true. I didn't like thinking about that too much.

We sat in silence for a while, driving and taking corners, until we were almost home. Then Larry said, "You know, you don't have to have a girlfriend at all."

I didn't know what to say to that, so I just said, "No?"

"No. You don't need to do what everyone else does. They're not your boss. You don't need to conform to everything everyone else is doing."

That reminded me of what God told me this afternoon. What was it? Something like, "You can't follow what everybody else is doing. You have to act counter to the culture. Jeff, I'm calling you to stand out. Be different. Play by a different set of rules, my rules." I thought that it would make the conversation less awkward if I agreed to something, so I said, "Yeah. In some ways we need to act counter to the culture. We can't follow what everybody else is doing."

Larry seemed very pleased with that answer. Not his usual jolly grin, but deeply pleased. He was nodding. "Jeff, that was a very good answer. I agree completely. Maybe there is hope for you after all." Then he said, "I just remembered something," and took out his phone. I thought about saying something about distracted driving, but didn't. He pushed some buttons then spoke into it, saying, "Remember to pick up butter." Then to me he said, "My digital assistant."

"Nice," I replied.

Arriving at our apartment, we parked and got out. As we set foot on the first step leading up to the door, Larry put out his hand in front of me. "Wait! Didn't your car get bombed?"

"Yeah. Yesterday."

"Maybe your apartment is next."

I didn't reply, due to the flood of fear and anxiety that swept over me.

Larry said, "I'll go check it out." He crept up the stairs, beeped himself in, then disappeared inside, but only for a second or two, because almost instantly he reemerged, running straight at me. He dove off the top step directly at me, and before I could react, my apartment exploded behind him.

5:29 PM

Larry landed on me, his body throwing mine down to the ground, while bits of cinder blocks flew around us. The boom was deafening, like the loudest firework times ten. And it was over in an instant. One moment I was standing on the first step, the next I was lying on the ground with Larry on top of me, my eardrums ringing, and my head aching from either hitting it on the ground, or the blast, or both.

As I pulled myself up, I noticed Larry was not moving, and he was bleeding from his head. Having an unconscious body on top of me spooked me so much, I pushed him off, and jumped to my feet. I may have still been a little groggy, but this shot of adrenaline was enough to counteract it, at least for now. I stared at Larry's bloody, still body lying on the ground, then I looked up at my apartment building. It had a hole in the side of it, and I could see right into my bedroom.

Then it occurred to me that the bomber might still be around, so I whipped my head around, looking for anything suspicious, and found something. In the bushes on the far side of the parking lot, I spotted movement and the reflection of the sun off of something that could only be interpreted as a silver antenna. Then it disappeared, and the person in the bushes disappeared too, presumably out the other side.

I should have run as far away from that person as I could, but I had seen something else besides the antenna.

Larry started moving, and he seemed OK for the moment, so I ran toward the bushes.

When I got there, I crawled through a small opening at the bottom. As soon as my head was out the other side, I turned and saw someone dressed all in black, sprinting away from me. I got up, and made chase.

Soon my pursuer was behind a building, and I was already breathing hard. It turns out programming doesn't automatically put your body in shape. I kept going, but not for long. A few strides later, I stopped and tried to recover my breath. I couldn't see the person anymore, anyway.

But then I heard an engine roar to life. That must be the get-away car getting away. I turned and started back to my place, but I could still hear the vehicle's engine on the other side of the building. Why wasn't it leaving? Then it occurred to me. Maybe there was no way back to the road from there. Maybe the very place I was standing was the only way out of this place. I looked around. The building was on my left, and there were some small trees on my right. I was in the bottleneck. If this car wanted to escape, it would have to come through me. I hoped it wouldn't actually do that.

Then I saw it. It was a light blue Dodge Charger. It looked dangerous. No doubt the driver was also dangerous. And it was driving straight toward me, very fast, engine revving.

I quickly reassessed what had just happened. A large vehicle was on a collision course to break both my legs or kill me. It was driven by someone who probably just blew up my apartment and may have just killed a guy. My brain told me that standing here was very dangerous and that I should move out of the way.

But another part of my brain said I was wrong, that the driver would stop and not hurt me. Then these two sides started fighting with each other, and they finally decided that it was a matter of probability. How sure was I that I saw what I really saw? Not a hundred percent sure, but quite sure. By now the car was halfway here. If I was only ninety-nine percent sure I saw what I did, that means there is only a one percent chance of serious injury here. I should take that chance, so I stayed put. Then it occurred to me that I was actually playing Russian Roulette. If I had a gun that held a hundred rounds but only had one bullet in it, would I point it at my femur and pull the trigger? I looked at the car about to hit me. No, I probably shouldn't do that, and besides, this was very scary.

Just as I was about to launch myself out of the way, the car slammed on its brakes. I saw it was still going to hit me, so instead of jumping out of the way, I jumped up. I landed on the hood, my face up against the windshield that had come to a complete stop. The driver looked mad, opened the door, and swore at me, then shouted, "Jeff, will you please get out of the way?!"

After a few breaths to recover from what just happened, I said simply, "Hi, Veronica."

5:46 PM

A few months ago, a local criminal that turned out to be my father who left us long ago, sent one of his agents to penetrate Omniscient Technologies, to make it easier for him to steal secret information in emails, and sell it to the highest bidder. That agent pretended to be romantically interested in me, one of the software developers there, and I fell for it. I dared to have feelings for her at the time, but her cover was blown, she disappeared, and I never saw her again until just now.

It also so happened that this woman had long dark hair, just like in Cheryl's dream.

She stood with one foot on the ground and one in the car, and both arms crossed. "What do you want, Jeff?"

Still lying on the hood, I shrugged. "I just wanted to know how you're doing."

"I'm fine. Will you get off my car, please?"

I nodded toward the passenger's seat. "Can I come in?"

"No."

I said nothing, but just held on to the top edge of the hood, ready for whatever this car could dish out.

She rolled her eyes. "Fine. If it'll get you off."

I scrambled off the hood, and into the passenger's seat,

while she got back in, too.

"First of all," I began, "why did you just blow up my apartment?"

"Get out!"

"OK, if you don't want to answer that question, how about... can we drive back to my apartment? The guy I was with got hurt. We should see how he's doing."

Her hardened features softened a little. I guess she does have some compassion left, even though she just tried to kill the guy. Come to think of it, that didn't make sense. Why should she care about Larry if she just tried to kill him? She said, "I'll take you, if you promise to get out when we get there."

"I promise."

We started driving, then I said, "So, Veronica, how are you?"

"I'm fine, Jeff. You don't need to take care of me. I can take care of us myself."

"What are you doing for work?"

"None of your business."

"Well, someone must have paid you to do this. Did you blow up my car, too?"

"Do you want to get out right now?"

"You should stop working for whoever you're working for."

"I don't need your advice."

"You're a good person. You shouldn't be involved with these bad people."

"See, that's where you're wrong, wonderboy. I'm not a good person. I'm a bad person. I'm a bad girl who does bad things for money."

We would soon be back at my apartment. I reached into my pocket, pulled out an envelope, and dropped it between us.

"What's this?" she asked, while turning the last corner.

"This is a token of friendship."

"We're not friends."

"But we could be."

She leaned forward and strained to see the damaged apartment building. Larry was walking around.

She lurched the car to a halt. "Now, get out!"

"Do the right thing, Veronica," I got out and closed the door.

The Dodge Charger reversed, pulled a one-eighty, and took off down the street. I ran to see how Larry was doing.

5:51 PM

Larry was fine. He had some bruises and a few small cuts on the back of his head and body, but he was up and walking around, kicking pieces of bricks, and gazing up into my apartment. Other people had also assembled, bystanders who were naturally drawn to anything interesting.

"There you are," he said to me. "Where did you go?"

"I thought I saw something in the bushes. I might have found the person who did this."

"Really?! Wow! That would be something."

"How are you, Larry? You seem a little beaten up."

"Me? Oh, I'm fine. I've been beaten up more than this."

One of the bystanders who looked like a feisty old lady, got off her phone and announced, "The police are on their way." I think I've seen her before. She might live here too. I wouldn't know; I don't pay attention to other people.

Another woman, similar to that one, commented, "Why do we need the police, Esther? We need a builder to fix this hole in our apartment building."

"Because it was a terrorist attack, Agnes! It was attempted murder. We could have all died. There might be more bombs still in the building. We need the bomb squad."

"You're daft, Esther. You don't need a bomb squad when a

water heater blows. I've seen them blow. They look just like this. Besides, terrorists wouldn't blow up this building; there is no one of importance living here."

"Of course there is. Jeffrey lives here." She pointed to me. I had no idea anyone knew me. Maybe she watched the news that one day I was on. She probably has nothing else to do with her time.

"Coincidence," Agnes replied. "Don't blame the terrorists just because his apartment is above the utility room. And he prefers Jeff, not Jeffery. Honestly, Esther. You need to get your facts straight."

"If you don't believe me, the police can decide. They will be here any minute."

Larry turned to me, "See you later, Jeff. I'm taking off. I have stuff I need to do."

What?! "But the police will want to talk to you."

"I'll drop by the station when I have some time."

"Um. OK."

With that, he got back into his car and drove away. At the same time, a police car drove up from the opposite direction. The officers got out and looked around. They looked ready for business. "Did anybody witness what happened?"

I raised my hand.

Esther called out, "I sure heard it. And felt it. I called it in, officer. Thanks for coming so soon."

"I don't see why you came at all," added Agnes. "A simple boiler explosion is dangerous, but not illegal."

"A boiler explosion, huh?" the first policeman said. He looked almost disappointed.

"Don't listen to her, office," said Esther. "This was a terrorist act. There are probably other bombs in the building."

The man held out his hands. "OK, listen. Your boiler is probably on the first floor, right? And the damage is on floor two. It's clearly not a boiler explosion."

"Boilers always blow straight up," Agnes said. "Everybody knows that."

The second man said to the first, "I'll go check it out. You can start on the witnesses." Then he went inside.

The first man turned to me and said, "What did you see, sir?"

I said, "Well, Larry and I were coming home from work."

"Who's Larry?"

"A guy I work with. He also lives here."

"With you?"

I frowned. "No. I'm in 201. He's in 203."

He looked around. "Which one is Larry?"

"He's not here. He left."

"Why?"

I shrugged. "I don't know. He said he had things to do."

"I'll need his contact information. Do you have his phone number?"

"I could get it."

"Thanks. I'll need that. So what did you see when you got home from work?"

"Larry went inside while I waited outside..."

"Why did you wait outside? Why didn't you go in?"

"Well, he said that since my car got blown up, that maybe someone might try my apartment, too."

His expression changed when realization dawned on him. "Oh, it was your car that blew up the other day."

"Yes."

"And now your apartment." He looked and pointed at the building. "Was your room affected by the blast?"

"Yeah." I pointed. "That's my bedroom right there."

"I see."

Just then the second police officer came out and said, "The blast appears to be centered around this first suite. The utility room downstairs seems fine."

"I told you, Agnes. You never listen."

"It sounded like a boiler explosion to me. I've heard them before. It sounded just like it."

The two officers talked among themselves, then the first one announced, "OK listen up, folks! You can't stay here right now. We're going to get the building searched to make sure there are no more explosives."

Some people complained, but not many. I suppose they weren't eager to go back to a dangerous situation. I was one of them.

The officer said to me, "Listen, Jeff. There is a chance we will consider this an attempted murder. If so, it will get included in the same case as your car blowing up. Do you know who is heading that investigation?"

I suddenly felt very weak, but I answered anyway. "Yeah. Joseph Wakefield."

The man grinned. "Really?"

"Yeah. Do you... do you know him?"

He shrugged. "Everyone does." Then he added, "You need to go talk with him."

"OK."

"Good. Take care. We're going to finish up here. Don't enter the building until the police tape is down."

One man started putting up yellow police tape over the doors and the hole in the wall. The other went inside, perhaps to tell people to get out. I turned toward my car and remembered I didn't have one.

I was now down a place to stay as well as something to drive. But like any good IT professional, I had backups.

CHAPTER 6

6:21 PM

I walked down the street to the local mall to buy two slices of pizza from the Pizza-by-the-slice shop. It wasn't high-quality fare, but it kept the hunger pangs away.

Then I caught the bus to a nearly abandoned house near the edge of the city. It wasn't completely abandoned, because I came here from time to time to flush the toilets, open the windows, and walk through it to admire the luxury of it all. It was a huge three-story mansion. It was my dad's. He still owned it, even though he was sitting in jail. I had thought of moving in, but if he gets out for whatever reason, he'll want it back. And I don't mind my apartment. Well, maybe I mind it now.

The bus had come to a stop some distance away, and I had to walk a few minutes, but I finally came to the driveway of this place. I looked at the large trees on either side of the driveway. It was beautiful. I guess you can buy nice things if you steal, and cheat, and threaten to kill people. I was one of those people he tried to kill. I remember that. I also remember what I tried to do to him. I sighed. And now we're father and son, or at least trying to be. Or at least, he would like to be. I didn't exactly know where I was. But I think it's going in the right direction.

There were five steps up to the front door, and three

strides toward the knob. I laid my hand on it and let my brain talk to me. Or was it my heart? Whatever it was, it was reminding me of what already happened today, not that long ago. Whoever blew up my apartment surely knew about my dad, and why wouldn't he, or she, also rig this thing to blow?

I relaxed my grip on the knob, and placed my hand back at my side, continuing to stare at the knob a little longer. So far these explosions have been limited to stuff that is mine, so I should be good here in a house that isn't mine. But maybe this house is considered part of what's mine now. I don't think so, but it's not what I think. It's what he thinks. Or she. I thought about Veronica. Didn't she say she was a bad girl who does bad things for bad people? Or something like that? That means she is just working for the bad guy. So this guy she's working for—would he blow up this house? I looked to the side at the large window, then up and around, as if this would help me decide if this place was worth blowing up.

Then I turned to see if I could see anyone in the bushes. Yes, there were trees on the other side of the front lawn, but of course I couldn't see any people. I ambled some distance away from the house, keeping my eyes out for any movement. There was none. I walked toward the other side of the yard, around the garage, but I couldn't see anyone there either. I should probably stop looking, because I'll never see anyone anyway.

Then I spotted a window on the side of the garage. I went and peeked in. There was nothing out of the ordinary, of course. It's not like I would find a chemistry lab inside or something. But I did notice that the window was full of spider webs. Obviously nobody cleans this place. Oh, but I guess that's my fault now. Then I noticed that the window was not latched completely. If it wasn't for the spider webs, I might think somebody had broken in here, but that wouldn't be possible. I tried sliding one pane of the window, because it was one of those windows that slides to the side. It moved! I could just sneak in here instead of going in the front door. That would be a lot safer.

But since the window was a bit high, I went and found a lawn chair and brought it back. Then I could reach nicely. I slid the window open and jumped up, pushing off the chair which promptly fell over. This left me perched on my stomach on an open window. Then I noticed that the alarm was counting down. It was calling out "Fifty-three, fifty-two…" The window sensor must have still been engaged until I disengaged it just now.

In front of me might be another bomb. But I had to shut off the alarm, or the police might show up. Behind me, was a long drop because the chair got knocked over. But I don't mind if the police show up; there's nothing wrong with that. It's my house. Or maybe my dad didn't make his alarm automatically call the cops. Maybe he would make it call someone else. That thought got me going.

I pushed myself through the window, and held on with one hand while my body fell not very gracefully inside, and I landed on my side on the concrete floor. "Thirty-seven, thirty-six.."

I ran for the alarm controls, squinting my eyes, knowing that at any second this house was going to explode, sending bits of wooden splinters at my unprotected body. I held up my arms around my head to protect it, but by then I was at the alarm control and punched in the numbers. It shut off, and I was left standing there, like someone in the middle of a minefield. Somehow I had survived, but anything around me might set off the real bomb.

I didn't even want to be there. I wasn't here for anything in the house. I was here for something in the garage.

I went back to the garage where I just came from, and stared at the reason I came here, my Honda Civic.

7:46 PM

It had been a few months since I parked this thing here, and I hadn't seen it since. I've been driving my dad's Mercedes. OK, I'll admit the Mercedes is a better car. It handles better, rides better, has better features, but... come to think of it, it's better in every way except one. It's in a million pieces, but this Civic is fully functional. That's why I'm here. I need a car, because there is something I need to do.

I walked over, and placed my hand on the driver's side door handle, but didn't pull, because I remembered the last time I went to my car. It blew up. Maybe this car in front of me has a bomb that is connected to the door handle somehow. It would have to be triggered somehow. I turned and looked at the garage window. I didn't like the idea that someone could be looking in. I felt like a loser for even thinking that someone could be looking in at me through this window, ready to remotely trigger a bomb. But like it or not, those thoughts were still there. I looked around and saw an old ping-pong table leaning against the wall, so I dragged it in front of the window. That made me feel slightly better.

Now it was just me and this car, which might have a bomb strapped to it underneath. Good thinking. I crouched down and looked under the car for any bombs. I couldn't see any. Then I turned on the light on my phone and took a closer look. I got on my back and stretched underneath as far as I could see. Still no car bombs, as far as I could tell. I wasn't a mechanic, so any one of these bits of metal under here could be a bomb, but it probably wasn't. I went around the entire perimeter of the vehicle this way. I got my backside very dusty, but at least I knew there weren't any bombs down there, or at least big ones. There might be some small guys hiding in the plumbing, but they were probably small and wouldn't make a big hole.

I placed my hand on the door handle, and was about to

pull when I thought of the back seat. I glanced in, and saw nothing, but there might still be something in the trunk or under the hood. I considered my options. I could pop the hood or the trunk, but doing that might set it off. I could just get in and drive away, but that might set it off too. I took a few deep breaths and thought about it. If you would plant a bomb in a car, you don't connect it to the hood release. That's common sense. I suppose by the same reasoning you wouldn't put a trigger on the trunk.

That left the door. Would you put a trigger on the driver's side door? You absolutely would. So I walked around to the passenger side door, and pulled on the handle. A fraction of a second after the door cracked open, and I saw the interior light go on, I knew I made a mistake. What better thing to trigger a car bomb than the interior light or accessory power? I held up my hands over my face to brace against the force of the impact, and stumbled backwards, tripping over a stray box of something. I landed on the floor, in the fetal position, covering my head like a shield. I lay there for a few seconds before I realized I was not dead. I wiggled my toes and hands to verify they still worked. Yup, I still had them, so I spread myself out on the concrete floor like a starfish, trying to catch my breath. The adrenaline rush of almost dying so often was exhausting.

Finally I spoke out loud, "God, are you there?"

The word "always" came to my mind, so I continued. "There might be a bomb in my car, and I don't want to die. What should I do?" Then I imagined him standing with me, but my imagination showed a man dressed in shining white standing next to my car, and these words came to me. "Fear is keeping you from taking action. Come take action." And I imagined the man gesturing toward the inside of the car.

I stood up. "Am I going to die?"

"Everybody dies eventually. Even Jesus died. Do you think you're better than Jesus?"

"I mean today. Will I die today?"

"If you do, you'll be with me, and you'll be a lot better off than you are here."

"You're not going to give me a firm commitment, are you?"

"I'll commit to you that I will always be with you, Jeff, no matter what happens. I will always be with you. I will always love you. I will always be your father, and you will always be my son and my friend. No matter what happens, even if you live or die, I will never leave you or abandon you. I AM with you always."

Those words softened my heart enough that I could crawl into the car from the passenger side, and sit in the driver's seat with the key in my hand. I looked over and imagined God sitting in the passenger seat. He was at peace and smiling, and motioning for me to turn the key.

I took a deep breath and as I let it out, I turned the key.

The car started.

I pressed the garage door opener clipped to my visor, waited for the door to open, then backed out. As I was leaving my dad's place, I said out loud, "Thanks," and felt his response of "Any time."

8:35 PM

Stony Mountain Penitentiary was old, and large, and could be mistaken for a parliament building, if it wasn't for the large wall, towers, and razor wire. It housed maximum, medium, and minimum security inmates. My dad was in minimum, because he wasn't violent. That made it easier to visit him, but it still took a while to get through all the levels of security, including being sniffed by a large dog that I imagined would take a bite out of some part of my body that didn't want to be bitten by a large drug-sniffing dog.

I was dropped off in the same medium-sized room I'd been

in before. The rug was worn, and the styles of the decor were many years old. But it had a coffee maker, so I helped myself. It wasn't quite the worst-tasting coffee in the world, but very close.

The door opened and a guard came in, bringing my dad. The guard glanced around the room, as if looking for people with guns or something, then left.

My dad stood there, wearing orange and a smile on his face. It wasn't one of those slick smiles from someone trying to sell you something. He looked happy, at peace, which always amazed me. It was as if going to jail was the best thing that ever happened to him. He used to be a bad man, but now he seemed gentle and kind. He would tell you it was because he became a Christian. He was probably right.

"Hi, Jeff," he said. "It's good to see you again."

"Hi, Dad."

We sat down. "How's Mom?" he asked.

I shrugged. "Fine, I guess."

"How are you?"

I didn't answer right away.

He continued. "Jeff, is something wrong? Is there trouble again?"

"Ah..."

"Tell me."

"My car blew up."

He frowned. "Who did this?"

I shook my head. "I don't know. I was hoping you'd have some ideas."

He kept on frowning until he did something I didn't expect. He hit the table with his fist, swore, and got up to walk around. So much for being a nice Christian. Then he added, "Sorry for my language," but he was still mad.

I said, "So, does that mean you know, or you don't know?"

"Well," he replied, "It could be anybody." That didn't make

me feel any better. "Maybe Max." Max was Dad's henchman who always hated me. "But he probably doesn't have the connections, nor the money. It could be Yash Nagi. He would have the connections, and the money, but he doesn't seem like the revenge kind of guy." Yash did try to kill me, so I'm not sure I agreed with that one. "Maybe one of Yash's guys."

Now I got curious. "You can have connections in prison?"

"Oh, of course. There's a whole… network of.. evil going on in this place. Every drug dealer, weapons dealer, thug, you name it, knows somebody, who knows somebody."

"Aren't you still in that network? Couldn't you find out who it is?"

"I'm out of the network. Everyone is scared I'll rat on them, now that I'm a Christian."

"Isn't there some sort of Christian network?"

"God does have a group of people that stay close, yes."

"In prison?"

"Of course. Everywhere."

I wasn't sure about everywhere. I didn't have a network of Godly people in my life. There was Cheryl of course, but not like a whole network of people. Come to think of it, it might be nice to belong with a bunch of like-minded people. Then a thought dropped into my mind that said, "When you share my email address, you'll find a God network." And in that moment, I seriously considered doing it.

And then I realized I wasn't paying attention to my dad, so I said. "Sorry, what did you say?"

"I said it might Vesuvius."

"Who's that?"

He faced away from me, looking up, as if not wanting to believe what he was saying was real.

"He, or she, was the one man, or woman, or whatever, that held us all together."

"You and Nagi?"

"Yes, and every other criminal in the area."

"So he had connections on the network?"

"He was the network."

"What do you mean?"

"I mean I'm not sure he even existed as a single person.. I've never seen his face. He might be a committee, or a corporation, or a ghost."

"Do you think he wants to kill me?"

He turned to look me in the eyes, then slowly nodded his head. "He wants you dead. You're bad for business."

I suddenly felt tired. "Someone who doesn't exist is trying to kill me."

"I'm sorry, Jeff." Then my dad came over and put his hand on my back, probably the most affectionate thing he's ever done to me, and despite the fact that he had done a lot of evil in his life to me and my mom and other people, and despite the fact that I wasn't sure if I had fully forgiven him for this, I had to admit, this little bit of affection felt very good. I was surprised by how good it felt. I was surprised that there was still a large part of my heart that longed for affection for my dad. I thought I was all grown up, but this part of me still existed. And maybe that was OK.

From my heart, I said, "Thanks, Dad."

This much emotion was probably overwhelming for both of us, so he backed away and we gathered ourselves together again.

"Have you been to the police?" he asked.

I nodded, "Yeah. And I got my old car from your house, since your Mercedes is gone."

"Maybe you should stay with a friend until this blows over. Sorry, maybe that was a bad choice of words. Do you have a friend you can stay with?"

"Yeah. Maybe Scott."

My dad smirked. "Yeah. Scott can take care of himself, and

you too."

I stared at him as if he had a story. He continued. "Did I ever tell you about the time your friend Scott disarmed me of a gun I was pointing at him in a car?"

I scowled. "No. You never told me that. Neither did he."

"You can ask him about it this evening. But that was the old me, I guess. I'm still not sure who the new me is, but I'm finding out."

"Is the new you kind?"

"I might be, yes."

"Generous?"

"I have my moments, yes."

"Honest?"

He sighed. "I'm trying, Jeff, but I lived a long life with a lot of secrets." Then he looked at the floor, as if ashamed. "There is something I've never told you before."

CHAPTER 7

8:54 PM

He sat down at the table with me and leaned forward. Then he leaned back. Then he sat up. "I... When I left your mother, I never expected to return. I didn't live like I was faithful to her."

I looked over at the coffee maker. This news shouldn't surprise me. I would be more surprised if he claimed he was faithful to Mom. Still, it didn't feel good to hear.

He continued. "In fact, even when I was still with her, I... I got a woman pregnant."

I looked back at him. This was news to me. "Did Mom ever find out?" I asked.

"No! Of, course not. Nobody ever did. Until now. I'm great at my secrets, remember?"

"Did she... keep it?"

"I pushed her to have an abortion, but she refused."

"Good." I didn't usually add so much commentary, and spout my own feelings and opinions, but this caught me in a moment of weakness. Suddenly I felt like I had to defend a little brother. I've never had a brother. I was being hit by so many feelings.

"She refused, so I left her."

Typical. Just when I start to disrespect this man a little less, he tells me how disrespectful he is. Or "was," I guess.

"Remember, I'm not that man anymore." He looked hurt in his eyes. I had to believe him.

"So you abandoned more people?"

"Not entirely. I kept my eye on the kid."

"And?"

"And at the right time, I recruited her to come work for me."

"*Her*? Who? Who is this person? Do I know her?"

"Yeah, you know her. I used her to infiltrate Omniscient."

"Veronica?" My mouth hung open.

My dad nodded.

"She's my sister." It was more of a statement than a question, trying to get my brain to learn this new piece of information.

My dad nodded. "Half-sister."

My brain was busy processing, reliving every moment with her, like I've done a thousand times already, but now from a new angle. "You know, we almost kissed once."

He chuckled. "Yeah, I saw that. That was funny."

"It's not funny! It's... incest."

"Ah, it's just a little peck between brother and sister. It never went anywhere."

"Still." Now I felt betrayed all over again. "You know I saw her today."

That wiped the smile off his face. "What? Where? How... how is she?"

"I think she blew up my apartment."

"Your apartment, too?!"

"Did I forget to mention my apartment got blown up, too?"

"And you think Veronica did it?"

"Yes. I caught her with a radio-controlled something, and she ran from me, but I caught her."

He got up again and paced, running his hand through his hair, mumbling something.

"What did you say?" I asked.

"I said you have to rescue her."

"Rescue her? From who?"

"If she's working for Vesuvius, he will get rid of her as soon as he's done with her. He doesn't have staff. He deletes anyone who knows who he is. Maybe he found out somehow that she's my daughter and your sister. Maybe that's why he's using her. To get to us. And when he's done with her..." He drew his finger across his neck. "You have to save her, Jeff."

I agreed completely. "But how? That's why I'm here, to get some advice from you on what I can do. What can I do?"

He kept pacing, then stopped, and slowly shook his head. "Nothing."

9:34 PM

I stood at the front of my car, leaning on the hood, one hand behind me, and the other holding a Dairy Queen vanilla ice cream cone. The white stuff was melting and running down the cone, onto my hand, then onto my shirt. Once in a while I remembered that I was holding it and licked at something, but most of the time I was staring off at nothing. The parking lot was right off Regent Avenue, where four lanes of cars make a cacophony of noise. I hoped the site of traffic and the noise of people could help the thoughts in my brain to calm down. There was too much to think about, but the thoughts kept coming. I couldn't even list everything going on up there. And now my hand was a sticky mess, but that was inconsequential.

I knew what I had to do. I had to seek God, to hear from him, to see him, to come into his presence. With the utmost strength, I caused my eyelids to relax and close, and tried to open the eyes of my spirit. The picture that immediately came to me was shocking. In my imagination, I saw God sitting cross-legged on the hood of my car, right next to me, licking a cherry chocolate ice cream cone, and loving it. I jerked my eyes open and looked there, but of course that half of the hood was empty. It was just my imagination.

I closed my eyes again, and imagined him next to me again. He was still there, licking away, fully enjoying life. "Hey, Jeff!," I imagined him saying. "This is good stuff. You should have some."

I opened my eyes again, saw nothing but me on the hood, but this time I shoved a mouthful of vanilla onto my tongue, then got back into it. Even with my mouth full, I could talk with my mind. I said to him, "I took a bite."

He replied, "Good. You took a step. Now you need to take another step."

"What step?" I almost chuckled.

"Ask Scott if you can go to his place. You need a place to sleep."

I added that to the pile of other worries on my heart, which was a growing list. I pulled one out at random. "I have to save my sister."

"You can't do that today, can you? Don't worry about that now, because today has enough worries of its own. Give it to me. Let me handle it. I'll do what I can do, and you do what you can do."

"What can I do?"

"You can lick the melted ice cream off your hand, because it's getting sticky."

I opened my eyes and stared at my hand, the soggy cone it held, and the blob of white on it. Maybe he was right. Maybe I can't do any of that now. But I can eat an ice cream cone. So I did, and soon it was done, and then I licked my hand clean, because I could. Then I wiped the spots off my shirt with the napkin that came with the cone. It didn't get everything, and my hand was still a bit sticky, but at least I had done it. I had accomplished something. Now I can take another step.

I pulled out my phone and found Scott's number. Before I dialed, I rehearsed what I was going to say in my mind, so I wouldn't have to do it in real time while talking. I hit the button and soon Scott said, "Hey, Jeff, what's up?"

"Hi, Scott. If you're not busy this evening, do you think I could spend the night at your place?"

"Pfff, sure, I guess. Why?"

"My ah... apartment has a large hole on one side."

"What? Oh, dude, did the bomber strike again?"

"Yeah."

"Are you OK?"

"Yeah, I guess."

"Of course. You got a car, or should I pick you up?"

"I got my Civic back. I'll be right over."

"Got it. See you soon, buddy."

"Thanks. Bye."

"Bye."

I pocketed my phone, took a deep breath, and let it out slowly. For some reason, deep inside, it felt good to be getting together with a friend. Living life on my own was tiring. I felt myself relaxing already, just thinking about sitting around with Scott. I started the car, and drove off the parking lot.

_10:21 PM_

"Wow," Scott said for the thirteenth time that evening. I was telling him everything about my apartment, and what my dad said about Vesuvius, and Veronica, who was my sister.

Scott leaned forward on his recliner while I sat back and relaxed on his black leather sofa, sipping a drink. He had made room for me by pushing away papers, books, empty boxes, and a few items of women's clothing. "Oh, how did your date go?" I asked.

Scott waved his hand and then thumbed down. "It didn't

go anywhere."

"It happens."

"Turns out she was one of those religious types–didn't want to have any fun."

I didn't say anything, because I feared I was one of those religious types.

"Speaking of fun, how's it going with you and... what's her name?"

"Cheryl."

"Cheryl! Are you two having fun together?"

I shrugged. "It's going very well. We enjoy each other's company."

"Yes, but you know. Are you enjoying each other in other ways?" He smirked.

I shifted in my seat, wondering what to say. I finally decided on, "No."

"Why not?" He was genuinely curious.

"Well... ah..." I looked, but he was still staring at me, wondering why in the world a girlfriend and boyfriend wouldn't get into bed together. "I... I guess... it doesn't... feel right."

"What do you mean? You're losing interest in her?"

"No! I... I love her."

"Then what's the problem?" He leaned back and put his hands behind his head, waiting for me to explain this.

I sighed. "OK. It's like this. When I think of sleeping with Cheryl, part of me feels really good."

"I'll bet it does."

"But part of me doesn't."

"What part is that?"

"Um... it's something else. It's something inside of me."

"Your soul?"

"I don't know what to call it. Soul? Spirit? Conscience?"

"A spirit guide?"

"No... well, maybe? Whatever it is, it doesn't like it."

"Spirit guides can be dangerous things. They're not good for you."

"If that's what it is, mine is good. He is kind. He is gentle. He is full of love."

"He is full of love but doesn't want you and Cheryl to love each other?"

I smiled. "He loves the idea of Cheryl and me loving each other with friendship love, just not sexual."

"Why not?"

"It's because we're not married yet."

Scott didn't reply right away, then finally he just said, "I wonder about you sometimes, Jeff."

Then he did something that would change the course of events drastically. He sat next to me and turned on his television on the wall to watch some YouTube.

10:35 PM

"I watch this guy because he's funny," Scott said, as he slid himself lower on the sofa, so his head was resting on the back.

The video opened with a man rowing a boat on the open waves, some distance from the shore where a giant cliff overlooked the sea. He said, "You can probably guess from the Orkney Islands behind us what today's episode is about." He had a strong Scottish accent. "And if you guessed quantum mechanics, you'd be right." Scott snickered.

The scene changed to the man inside a restaurant, with the view of the ocean out a window beside him. "I'm Smith MacNeil, and you're watching TechnoSomething, the show where I usually talk about something." He took a sip of coffee. "In this today's episode we find out that TK15 is broken. Maybe. It depends. Probably not, but there is a chance it is utterly, completely susceptible to a little trick using quantum computers."

I turned to Scott. "We use TK15. We switched to it because our other encryption algorithm wasn't secure enough."

"Don't believe this guy. It's just for show. It's clickbait. We'll find out soon enough." Scott said those words, but he didn't look convinced. He was hoping he was right, just like I was.

Smith took a sip of tea. "Now the first thing you'll say is, 'But Smith, quantum computing is just a myth. It's a billion-dollar industry, and has nothing to show for it and never will.'" He turned fully to the camera. "To which I would say…" He took a chug from an orange can with the words, "Iron Bru" on it, pointed at the camera, and almost yelled, "That's where you're wrong! It's a trillion-dollar industry with almost nothing to show for it." He finished off the scene by sucking on a straw in a glass of water, but with great emotion.

"This guy's awesome," Scott remarked. I didn't say anything.

The scene showed him jacking up his car while monologuing. "Now there are a handful of companies that actually sell time on their hardware–'Quantum computing as a service', so to speak. But there aren't many of them. And the services available aren't the miracles that everyone has been promising."

Smith next appeared leaning over slightly, with the camera low and nothing but sky behind him. He was wearing a large fake mustache and an old Derby-style hat. "With quantum computing, you will be able to crack DES in 5 minutes, AES in 4 minutes, and MD5 virtually instantly. Nothing is safe. You can kiss your privacy goodbye. Have you heard of RSA? TSL? VPS? All gone!"

Back to jacking up the car. "Don't believe that fake news." He stopped jacking, reached under the tire and picked up a smartphone underneath it and put it in his pants pocket without breaking eye contact with the camera. Then he started letting the car down. "However, there is a small edge case that an analog quantum computer can exploit. It can use a property of an elliptical curve cryptography system to gain an advantage in deciphering it. I'll spare you the math and physics..."

"See?" said Scott. "That means it's bunk."

"...but let's just say I wouldn't put my money in a bank that uses TK15." The scene cut back to Smith on a row boat on the water, eating a hot dog. "At least that's the theory... I've never seen it happen in real life to real people with real files... but in theory it could, so I'd stay away from it... maybe if I got my hands on a quantum computer, I'd demonstrate a proof of concept... but until then, I hope you enjoyed this piece of TechnoSomething. I'm Smith MacNeil." The camera panned back, showing him trying to row back to shore.

"You can't even buy quantum computers yet," said Scott. "They don't exist."

"So it's only theoretical? And will never happen?" I asked.

Scott paused a little too long for my liking, but then replied, "I wouldn't worry about it. We're doing everything right." Then he stood. "Good night, buddy. See you tomorrow."

"Good night."

He went to another room and closed the door, leaving me alone on the sofa. I found a little blanket and lay down under it, thinking I would sleep uneventfully until morning.

2:00 AM

I woke up to a thought landing heavily on my mind, so heavily I woke up from it. It said, "I have an assignment for you."

I sighed and looked at the time, then sighed again. Surely this could wait until the morning, but the thought came louder. "I have an assignment for you."

I slowly pulled myself into a sitting position and said, "Hello, God. Here I am. What can I do for you? At two in the morning?"

The words in my mind shifted to three words, "Send the email."

"What?"

"Send the email."

"Now? It's the middle of the night!"

"Send the email."

"I'm tired. I'll do it in the morning."

"Send. The. Email."

I looked over at the spot on the sofa that was still warm and inviting, but I knew that at this point, going back to sleep now would be an act of deliberate disobedience. Fine. I took out my phone and started composing. After a lot of anxiety, reflection, false starts, backtracks, and self-doubt, this is what I finally typed in on my little on-screen software keyboard.

From: Jeff Davis

To: Scott Stark, Doug Grimm, Garth Fonte

Subject: God's Email Address

Hey guys. I know this is going to sound crazy. It even sounds crazy to me, but it actually happened. A while ago, the lady who looked after the plants gave me a piece of paper that said, "god@heaven" on it. She said it was God's email address and that I could talk to him whenever I wanted to. Of course I thought she was crazy, and I even explained why it wouldn't work–it was missing a top-level domain. But then I tried it, and it seemed to work. I sent email messages to this address, and for a while they would all come back with a real reply. They don't always anymore, for me, but a while ago I got one that said I should give you three the email address, so that's what I'm doing. I don't know what will happen if you send something to it, but here you go. God's email address is god@heaven. Try it. See you in the morning.

My finger paused over the Send button. Somehow I knew that if I tapped the button, my life would never be the same. What had God said? He didn't want just one server, he wanted a whole network. I think God might be getting his network. Before I tapped the button, I closed my eyes once more and imagined God with me. I could see his smile shining down on me, and could feel his love radiating into me, his son. I tapped the button then lay down, wondering if I could get back to sleep again.

CHAPTER 8

4:00 AM

"Jeff!" I heard Scott's voice, but my eyes were still shut. "Jeff!" Then I felt him shake me and I awoke with a start.

"What?!" I asked, looking around, wondering where I was. It was dark, but I remembered I was at Scott's place.

"What is this?" he demanded.

"What's what?"

"This email address. Where does it go? And what is coming back to me?" He seemed almost distraught, not his usual carefree self.

I shook my head. "I don't know."

"What do you mean you don't know? You sent me this email two hours ago. What is this all about?"

"I told you everything I know."

He shook his head, and kept shaking it. "No. You... this... this is impossible."

"I agree that under normal circumstances, it would be impossible, yes."

"But?"

"I don't understand it either. The only conclusion I can reach is that if it is really God, God can do whatever he wants to."

"Including sending email?!"

I shrugged. "Whatever he wants means whatever he

wants."

Scott stood there with no words to say, so I broke the silence. "I was afraid it wouldn't work."

"Well something's working."

"Is it? Would you like to share what you got?"

He sat down and ran a hand through his already disheveled hair. "What? Should I just read it to you?"

"Sure."

He looked through stuff on his phone. "Um..."

"What's the first thing you said to him?"

"The first email I sent?"

"Yeah."

"It just said, 'Hello'"

"And the response?"

"It said, 'Hi Scott.' That was... spooky." He looked up at me. "This is a bot, isn't it?"

"No. I checked. Believe me. I checked everything."

"Then how do you explain it?"

I shrugged again. "The only thing that explains it is almighty God using email." Scott looked distraught to me, so I asked, "What's wrong?"

"It's just that... in that case, I don't know if I want to pursue this."

"Why not?"

"Because I don't feel like being chewed out some more. My dad yelled at me all the time until I finally left home. I don't need God to start yelling at me too, and believe me, I've done plenty to get yelled at by a holy, pious God. No thank you. God and I wouldn't get along."

"I haven't noticed God ever yelling at me."

"You're different. You're a choir boy."

"At least give him a chance. You could send him an email saying you don't want to get yelled at."

"Fine. I'll do that." He punched his thumbs at his phone

for a minute, then said, "There. I sent it."

"What did you say?"

"You really want to hear it?"

"Yup."

"OK. I said, 'If you really are God, you won't be interested in me, because I've done some bad stuff. And if you're just going to cuss me out for it, I'm not interested in that either. Have a good life.'"

"You're honest. That's good."

"The reply just came in."

"I'd love to hear it."

"Fine." He started reading. "It says, 'Dear Scott. I'm not going to cuss you out. I'd give you a big hug if I could. Fathers need to love their sons, like I love you. If your dad was more like me, he would have told you he loved you every day, and given you hugs, and played with you in the sandbox, and done all the things a dad should do. I wish he would have. It's what I would have done with you, Scott, my son.'"

The warmth in my heart overflowed into a smile on my face. I loved listening to these words. They were so full of love. But Scott wasn't smiling. A number of emotions played out on his face, and the winner was hardness of heart. He typed more.

"What are you saying?" I asked.

He replied, "I said, 'It's too late.' And the reply is back already. It says, 'It's never too late. I've been loving you every day of your life, waiting for the day you would finally turn to me. You don't have to clean yourself up to come to me, Scott, my son. Come to me dirty. Come to me with all your smelly sin, and let me help you with it. Come to me like a child who has fallen in the mud and came running to his mom to clean him up. Come to me, Scott. Let me wrap my loving arms around you just the way you are. We have your whole lifetime to get you cleaned up, and strong on your feet, but for now just come to me.'"

The hardness on Scott's face was gone, and softness had taken its place. He said, "I don't know what to do."

"You could go back to your room, and carry on the conversation. Ask him anything you want, and listen for his answer. Just start talking. And start listening."

He nodded. "Yeah. See you tomorrow, Jeff."

"Good night."

He trudged back to his room, his thumbs already typing a reply.

Before going to sleep, I prayed. "God, please take hold of Scott's heart and pursue a relationship with him." Then I took my own advice and listened for a response. The words that came to my mind were, "It would be my pleasure."

Thursday, 7:30 AM

I awoke with a headache and didn't feel like talking. No doubt Scott's sofa was a terrible bed. I sat at one end of the table, chewing toast, while Scott sat at the other end, eating sugary cereal out of a bowl, in his underwear. He wasn't talking either, but it wasn't because of a bad mood. Even though his eyes were a bit bleary, he seemed at peace and even happy.

He seemed lost in thought, and every few seconds would type something into his phone, and smile at the response. If I were in a better mood I would ask him what he was doing, but I didn't feel like talking. He was probably talking with God. Go ahead then, talk. It's none of my business anyway. At least I didn't think so. But maybe they're talking about me.

"Are you talking about me?" I managed to ask.

"What?" He seemed startled. "Oh! Yes, actually." And that's all he said. Fine with me. Let them talk. I kept eating.

At one point Scott looked at the time, swore, and ran out to his room, but before he got there, he caught himself and said, "Sorry!". Did he just apologize for swearing? He's never done that before. Maybe this God of mine is having an affect on him, too. That didn't take long. We'll know it works if he stops sleeping around with all the girls.

Soon he was back, dressed, and heading to the door. "We gotta run, buddy!"

I walked with him to the door, out the door, then we were soon seated in his red Mustang, roaring down the road as if we were late and might get fired. Yes, we were late, but no, we probably wouldn't get fired.

As he wove around cars, Scott said, "You know what the weird thing is?"

"What?" My headache was going away.

"He doesn't tell you everything."

"Why not?"

"I mean he could; he just chooses not to."

"Why?"

"He explained it this way..." These words sounded strange in my ears. I was not used to other people talking about how God was talking to them. That was a thing I usually experienced myself. He continued. "A mom could come home with a bag of candies and hand them out evenly to all her kids."

"Yeah?"

"Or she could give them all to one kid, and tell him to share equally."

I thought about that. "Why would a mom do that?"

"Duh! To teach one kid to share what he has, and teach the other ones to receive. Sorry, I didn't mean to be condescending. I didn't understand it either myself the first time."

"OK."

"So the reason God doesn't tell one person everything is to get him, me, or you, to go to someone else. It encourages interdependence, sharing, friendship."

"God wants us to be friends?"

"Yes! Exactly! See, I have a house, and I shared it with you."

"Oh yeah, thanks for that, by the way. Thanks for the sofa."

"Oh yeah! No problem! Any time!"

Scott seemed happy. Good. Let him be happy. It was good to be in the presence of happy people. Come to think of it, that's true. I sat back in the passenger seat and relaxed. It wasn't a bad day at all.

8:07 AM

Scott turned right into the staff kitchen, presumably to pick up some coffee. I turned left, went down the hall, and into our corner room.

Garth's little white board was empty, and when I looked at the man himself, he looked terrible. His eyes were almost bloodshot. "Good morning, Garth," I ventured.

He kept staring at his screen with a purpose. "Don't talk to me," he replied. Even his voice sounded extra gravelly.

I turned the other way toward Doug, who swiveled around toward me. "I don't think he slept well," he said, "after receiving your email at night."

I turned back to Garth, who kept his back to me, but now also raised his hand up in a rude gesture as well. "But he doesn't want to talk about it," Doug finished.

I wanted to ask Doug if he wanted to talk about it, but I just didn't have the courage. Hey, I did my part. I sent the email, like God asked me to. My part is done. I don't need to ask anyone what they thought of the email I sent.

Just then, Scott burst into the room and exclaimed, "Hey, what did you all think of that email that Jeff sent?"

He patted Garth on the back and said, "Did you try it, buddy? What did you think? Did you get a reply? It's crazy, isn't it?"

"Shut up."

"What? I thought you would love talking with God. You probably have a pile of questions a mile high you're just itching to ask him. You were probably up all night, just like the rest of us, talking away."

"I said shut up. I'm working. I don't have time for your petty chatter."

"Oh, it's like that, is it? The wildest thing that's ever happened to us, and you don't want to talk about it, huh? Well, the rest of us will, right here, right now." He turned to Doug. "Doug, did you try it?"

Doug kept a pleasant smile on his face, and slowly nodded his head up and down.

"What did you think? Did God say anything cool to you?"

Doug breathed in, then breathed out, then slowly nodded again.

"What? What did he say? Tell us."

Doug paused in thought, a sharp contrast between Scott's talkative enthusiasm. "Um... I think I'll pass on sharing right now. Perhaps what was said should remain between us, at least for now."

Scott seemed a little deflated. "OK... but you believe, right?"

"Believe what, exactly?"

"That... that this email is God's email address. You're really talking with him."

He shook his head, which startled me, until he spoke. "I can't think of any other way of explaining it. It's technically impossible to communicate with this email address, and I can't think of anywhere else the content could possibly come from." That sounded better.

"I know, right?!" Scott was still excited. He put his hands on his head. "It blows my mind."

At that, Garth exploded. He nearly yelled, "If you don't

keep your voices down, so I can work, I will have to take my work elsewhere." He stood up, grabbed his Dr. Pepper, and stormed out of the room.

Scott finally sat down and said, "What's his problem?"

"His eyes are bloodshot," I volunteered.

"If I had to guess," began Doug, "I would say that he has been up all night, ever since receiving Jeff's email, and he has been trying it out."

"And it didn't work?" asked Scott. "I assumed it worked for everybody."

"Oh, no," said Doug. "I suspect it worked perfectly well, and that's the problem."

"What?" asked Scott in confusion.

"We all know that Garth is a staunch atheist, and now he has irrefutable proof of God's existence, plopped down in his lap, but he simply can't deny easily everything he stands for so easily. His mind refuses to accept it. But at the same time, his mind must accept it, because I'm sure he has spent hours trying everything he can think of to explain it away somehow, and can't."

"When I first got God's email address," I began, "I tried everything I could think of, including opening a new email account with a company I had never heard of, on a different computer, and it still worked."

"I'm sure Garth has done all those things and more."

"Poor guy," said Scott. "He should just give in."

"He might," said Doug.

I swiveled back to my computer to get to work, but Scott and Doug kept on talking. I tried concentrating on what was in front of me, but I kept hearing pieces of conversation. Someone said, "Did you try a different email client?", then "Yeah," and "This guy talks like nothing I've ever heard." "Not... what's the word... distant", "Yeah. Close. Personal", then "Did you give the address to anyone else?", "No, hadn't thought of it.", "Maybe we could now," "Nigel." "Yeah." "OK"

8:29 AM

My curiosity got the better of me, so I turned around to see the two guys leaving the room. But before Scott got out the door, he spied Garth's empty whiteboard, so he snuck a marker from his desk and wrote something on it. Then he disappeared around the corner.

I didn't want to be around when someone else tried God's email address. The thought filled me with anxiety. But I was also wondering what would happen. Scott would be able to handle anything embarrassing, so I got up and tagged along. I stood behind them in our boss Nigel's office. Nigel was a bit younger than you would expect a technology boss to be, but he was a nice guy and we all liked him.

Nigel looked up and smiled. "What's up, guys?"

Scott said, "Could you just check something for us in Omniscient?"

"Ah. OK. What do you want me to do?"

"Just go to start writing an email."

Nigel clicked a few times, then said, "OK."

Scott said, "Please type in the To field, 'God At Heaven'".

"Just like that? I don't think that's a real email address."

"That's what we're testing."

Nigel typed on his keyboard. I noticed it wasn't as loud and clackety as Scott's. Then he said, "OK. Should I try sending something here?"

"Yes, anything, like 'Hi.'"

Nigel typed some more, then clicked a button. "It said, 'Invalid email address.'"

Scott said, "OK, thanks Nigel."

"Just that? Couldn't you test that anywhere?"

"Yeah, we're just doing some hallway testing."

"I know what hallway testing is, Scott. This isn't that."

"Yeah, well, whatever you call it, it worked. Thanks for your time." He turned and ran, with Doug right behind him.

I tried to go too, but Nigel called out, "Jeff!"

Oh no. He's going to ask me about God's email address, and I'm going to either try to avoid it or admit to being weird. I turned to face him.

He said, "You, of course, are familiar with TK15?"

I breathed a sigh of relief, then shrugged. "I guess so."

"Have you heard any rumors that it isn't as safe as we think it is?"

Then I remembered the YouTube video we watched. "I may have heard rumors about TK15 and quantum computers, but I don't know how true they are."

"Would you like to look into it?"

"OK."

"Thanks."

Then I left and found the other two, who were gathered outside Cheryl's cubicle.

Cheryl was saying, "God at heaven, you say, eh? Hmm... You think that will work?"

Scott replied, "We don't know if it will work. That's why we'd like you to try it."

"What do you think will happen?" she asked.

"Um... guys?" I tried to interrupt, but it wasn't working.

"We're just testing something," said Scott.

"What are you testing?" asked Cheryl again, the slightest trace of a grin on her face. "A feature in Omniscient, or this specific address?"

"A feature of the software," said Scott.

"Guys?" I tried interrupting again, but was ignored again.

"So I could use any email address then?" asked Cheryl.

"We'd like you to please try this one. Just to see what happens."

"What happens when you use it?" Cheryl asked.

"We're on a different version. We'd like you to try."

"Guys!" I said again, loud enough to get their attention. Scott and Doug looked at me. "This is the plant lady."

They stared at me in confusion.

I lowered my voice so nobody else could hear the crazy words coming out of my mouth. "This is the person I got God's email address from."

Then they understood.

"Oh!" exclaimed Scott. "So you know what we're all up to here."

She smiled and nodded. "You got his address from Jeff? He finally told you?"

"Yeah. He sent us an email last night."

"This night," corrected Doug.

"Whatever," Scott replied. Then he said, "Hey! Does anyone else here know the secret?"

"No, I don't think so," Cheryl said.

I also shook my head.

"In that case, we need to have a meeting. Let's talk in the kitchen." Without looking back, Scott took off for the kitchen. Doug followed.

I shrugged at Cheryl, who stood up, and we both went to join them.

CHAPTER 9

8:52 AM

We found Scott and Doug huddled around a table at the far end of the kitchen, away from everybody else. Cheryl and I joined them.

"So what we have here," said Scott, "is like a gang. We're a gang."

"Like the Crips or the Bloods?" asked Doug, but I didn't know what he was talking about.

"No," said Scott.

"How about Hell's Angels?" I suggested, "That's a gang."

"That wouldn't be appropriate," said Cheryl. "We're more like Heaven's Angels."

"The opposite of Hell's Angels is Heaven's Demons," said Doug.

"We're not demons," said Cheryl.

"I might feel like a demon sometimes," said Scott.

"Closer to a demon than an angel," said Doug.

"We're not demons, and we're not angels," said Cheryl. "We're people."

"It's just a name," replied Scott.

"But names should be meaningful," I said, "just like picking variable names. We're programmers. We know that variables should accurately reflect what they represent."

"That's true," said Scott, "but still 'foo' and 'bar' are the most popular variable names, and they don't mean anything."

"In the Linux kernel, there's lots of profanity as variable names," added Doug.

"Our Omniscient code doesn't have profanity in it, does it?" asked Cheryl.

"No," said Scott, "but I once abbreviated the word 'seconds' as s-e-c-s, and got away with it."

"That's because nobody reads code out loud," said Doug.

"And it's a good thing we're using a garbage-collected language," continued Scott, "or I would have to free up memory after allocating it."

"Using the 'free()' function?" asked Doug.

"That's right. We'd have a lot of 'free(secs)' around here."

"Moving on!" interrupted Cheryl.

"Maybe we don't need a name at all," I said, taking out my phone. " I mean, the Linux kernel versions have names, and nobody uses them."

"Really?" asked Scott. "They have names?"

"Yes." I found the page I was looking for and started reading some. "For example, Linux 4.9 is 'Roaring Lionus'"

"That's not so bad," said Cheryl.

"It's not 'Lioness', it's 'Lionus'. Linus Torvalds probably named it after himself."

"Linus doesn't even pronounce his name 'Linus'." said Scott. "He pronounces it 'Linus.'"

"I've always pronounced 'Linus' as 'Linus'," said Doug.

"No, that's wrong," said Scott. "It's 'Linus'"

"'Roaring Lionus' isn't even bad," I said. "Version 4.3 was called 'Blurry Fish Butt'."

"Really?" said Cheryl.

"There's also 'Pink Farting Weasel,' and 'Holy Dancing Manatees, Batman!', and 'Jeff Thinks I Should Change This, But To What?'"

"That's a real name?" asked Cheryl.

"Yup, for version 2.6.22 release candidate 4."

Doug said, "We could call ourselves 'Scott Thinks We Should Have A Name, But What?'"

Scott replied, "And for short, we'll just call ourselves the 'But What's'"

Cheryl didn't like it. She said, "No." I also shook my head. She continued with, "If you guys aren't going to be serious, I have work to do."

"Of course we're serious, Cheryl," said Scott. "So serious, I'm going to send an email. Just hang on." He took out his phone and started poking and sliding his finger around, while muttering out loud, "Hey God, we're trying to think of a name. You want to give us one?" Then he put it down and said, "I expect a reply very soon." Then his phone played the email song and he checked it.

"What does it say?" asked Doug.

Scott held up his phone and said, "It says, 'Hi, Scott. It's always good to talk with you. Thanks for asking. Thanks for coming to me with your problems. I will help you with everything you bring to me. I will never abandon you or leave you. I'm always there for you, no matter what difficulty you face. I will always be your father, and you will always be my son." At that, Scott paused and took a breath. I suppose he wasn't used to receiving words at this heart level, and I don't blame him. When I first started hearing from God, my heart was very dry, and God's words of love often moved me to tears when they landed on the dusty soil of my heart. Now that he has filled my heart with soft love, I don't tear up anymore. I just say, "I love you, too," and mean it.

Scott continued reading. "As for your name, I have already given you everything you need to choose a good name. Your creativity comes from me. Your imagination comes from me. Everything good comes from me. It is your choice to put this creative imagination to work and think of a name. Remember that I gave Adam everything he needed, in the Garden of Eden, then I tasked him with naming the animals. You too, can name things."

"How about 'Fellowship of the Ring'?" Doug suggested.

"We don't have a ring," said Scott. "Maybe Jeff here needs to buy a ring."

It was a good thing I wasn't drinking coffee, or I would have coughed it up. I glanced at Cheryl who was looking at me with an expression I couldn't quite place. Needing to avoid any more awkwardness, I stood up and declared that Nigel had asked me to look into something and I had to go. Without looking back, I made my way back to my desk, and decided to research TK15 to see if our entire communication network was vulnerable to attack.

11:01 AM

I was wondering if I was going to get any real work done today at all. I had already just spent a few hours researching the TK15 encryption algorithm, elliptical curve cryptography systems, quantum computing with different numbers of cubits, and I finally had to begrudgingly admit that in theory it might be possible to crack TK15, given the right circumstances. Maybe after I told my findings to Nigel, I could get back to some real programming.

I got up to go tell Nigel, but that's when Cheryl came in.

"Jeff, I forgot to tell you earlier. We are invited to my parents' place this evening."

"OK."

She smiled. "Great!" Then, turning to Garth's whiteboard, she cocked her head and said, "What does this mean?" The whiteboard simply read, "418".

I said, "Scott wrote that. I think it's a reference to HTTP Response Code 418, which is, 'I'm a teapot'."

"What?"

"Yeah. It has to do with the Hyper Text Coffee Pot Control Protocol. When the client sends a request to the server to brew coffee, the server may return error code 418, which is 'I'm a teapot.'"

"You're not serious."

"I am. It's in the official spec."

"Is this for, like, smart coffee makers or something?"

"No, it was an April Fool's joke that somehow found its way into the official protocol."

"Ah, an April Fool's joke. That makes more sense."

"Yeah. I guess that's why Scott put it on the joke board."

"So, we'll see you this evening?"

"Yup!" I smiled. "Should I pick you up?"

She smiled. "Sure!"

"OK. I'll see you later."

Still happy, she left the room, and I went to see Nigel. I plopped down in a chair in his office and waited for him to acknowledge me. He was busy doing something on his computer. I didn't know what bosses did in their spare time. For all I know, he could be checking out prices of snowmobiles.

Then he looked at me, smiled, and said, "Hey Jeff! What can I do for you?" He was a pretty good boss.

I tried to form the words in my mind. I suppose I should have done that first before coming here. "I did the research into TK15, and given the right circumstances, in theory, it is probably possible to crack it easier with the right kind of quantum computer."

He frowned. "I guess we should change it before we get hacked. We've already made the news too much. I'll file an issue in our bug tracker. Would you like to get started picking a new encryption method? And pick something good this time."

I may not have been the guy who made the final decision to go with TK15, but I was on the committee, so I just said,

"OK".

"Thanks, Jeff. Oh, and one more thing. Can you help Ronja with setting up the new security software?"

"What new security software?"

"Security cameras and stuff. It's for physical security, not network access security."

I shrugged. "OK." So much for real work today–first this new security software, then more research. Oh well.

"Thanks."

I got up and went to find Ronja. She was in her cubical. "Hi Ronja," I said.

"Yes, hello Jeff. Nigel has agreed to let you help with the new software, yes?"

"Yes."

"Ah, good. Have you heard of this piece of software? It's called 'Security Tight'."

"No, I haven't heard of it."

"It is open source, and becoming popular with large organizations. It can be quite complex."

"I'll take a look at it."

"Thank you. Oh! I almost forgot. You will not have access to it from your computer, because you are on a different VLAN. We divided up each peripheral on the network to not have access to everything else, but for now I can give you access to the cameras and door locks."

"All that is on a separate network?"

"Yes, it is now."

"Now that Larry did his security audit?"

"Yes."

"Is he soon done?"

"He will probably finish today."

"Just in case the cameras and stuff are on the wrong network, maybe you should give me access to everything, so I can troubleshoot better."

"You want access to the Everything Network?"

Yes, the Everything Network, or the God Network, as I like to call it. "It would be easier to troubleshoot and set things up if I could easily connect to everything else."

"Hmm... yes... very well. I will connect you to this network. I will configure Security Tight to grant access to everyone coming in on this network. That way you don't need an extra password."

"OK, thanks."

"Then you will have access to Security Tight and everything else on that network, but I will still email you the IP addresses of the peripherals, and config file locations."

"OK."

"Good. If you have any questions, you may ask me."

"Yeah, I have a question. Why did they give it such a dumb name?"

"You don't like Security Tight?"

"No. It sounds... awkward."

"Well, can you think of something better?"

"Sure. How about Secure Tight? Or Lock Down? Or... Eye Spy?"

"I agree. Eye Spy might be a better name, but it already has a name. I don't think we will change it now." Ronja's phone vibrated and she looked at it, then knit her eyebrows. In distress, she looked at me and said, "My nephew, whom I am babysitting, has had an accident. I must go take care of it."

"OK."

"I don't have time to give you access to the correct network. I... I will give you the admin password for the network switch." She grabbed a pad of sticky notes and scratched some random-looking characters on it with a pencil and handed me the top piece. "Be responsible," she added, as she hurried away.

I stood there, looking at the paper, realizing I didn't even know where this switch was. But I could probably figure it out. Well, I had work to do.

11:54 AM

I stood in the lobby, next to the big glass door, head down, examining my phone. I wasn't checking email or on social media. I was logged into Security Tight. It was supposed to record an event to the log whenever this front door opened or closed. So far it wasn't working. It had taken me a few minutes of hunting down the right server on the right network, but I finally found it, and once my phone was on the right VLAN, I could connect like a charm. Being on the right network makes all the difference. Now it was just a matter of getting Security Tight to do what I wanted it to do.

"Try closing it and opening it again."

I looked over at who was speaking. It was the receptionist, Luanna. It looked like she was telling a joke, but I didn't get it.

"It's a joke. You know, since you're a computer guy."

I blinked. I still didn't get it.

"OK, the joke goes like this," she began. "An electrical engineer, a mechanical engineer, and a software engineer are driving along in a car, when the car suddenly dies. The electrical engineer says, 'It must be a wiring problem, with the battery or the fuses.' The mechanical engineer says,"We should check the timing belt." The software engineer says, 'I know, let's close all the windows, get out, get back in, and open all the windows again.'" Then she laughed.

Yeah, that wasn't bad. I chuckled too.

"Hey, what are you doing with the door, anyway?"

"I'm trying to get the new security software to work. The cameras work already. Here, I'll show you." I showed her my phone with the cameras playing their feed live. I waved up at a camera in the corner and we watched me waving on the phone.

"So when I think I'm alone and pick my nose, you'll be able to see it?"

"Yup. And it's recorded, too."

"Great."

Just then Garth entered the room, wearing a black t-shirt with red spots on it that resembled Darth Maul. He proclaimed, "I have been seeking the network administrator, but am told that she is currently out."

"Yeah. Something happened with her nephew," I said.

"In that unfortunate case, I am forced to speak with you, Jeff Davis, against my better judgment."

I sighed. Garth can be tiring to work with sometimes. "What can I do for you?"

"I require network access to a computer I have set up on the network. The following ports are all blocked. 25, 2525, 587, 465, 110, 143, 993, and 995."

I recognized some of those ports. They are used for email. "The only computer you can connect to for email purposes is our local Omniscient server. Nothing else."

"Why?!"

"For security reasons, the network is split into different VLANs..."

"I know what a VLAN is! And I know that you can put me on the right one." I paused to wonder how he knew Ronja had given me the admin password for the switch, but he continued. "I saw you configuring the switch to give yourself access to everything. As well as your phone."

I reflexively glanced down at my phone that was still displaying the feed from the security camera. "Um... yeah."

"So put me on that network, too."

"Um... Ronja told me to be responsible."

"She would do it for me. You should too."

My hands started sweating. I hated confrontation. "I think we should wait until she gets back."

"Which is when?"

"I don't know."

"You may be correct in that you don't know, but something you do know is how to get me onto that network."

Through the beating of my heart, I searched my brain for some words to respond with, but I couldn't find any, except, "Ah..."

But I was saved from my conflict with this large, angry man by my friend Scott who came whistling into the room. "Hey, Jeff! Wanna come for lunch? I got a hankering for pancakes."

The breath I was holding came out in the word, "Yup!". I stepped around the big guy and headed out the door with Scott. Then I noticed other people following us, including Larry. I groaned. I didn't want to go for lunch with Larry.

12:25 PM

Scott was almost done his Giant Apple Pancake, topped with cinnamon glaze. I wasn't as adventurous and settled for the Chocolate Banana pancakes, which came with Nutella, custard, whipped cream, and chocolate chips.

Besides us, there were also Doug, Larry, and Cheryl. I sat beside Cheryl of course. The talk around the table consisted mostly of what the big tech companies were up to, as well as the usual topics like cryptocurrency, quantum computing, and artificial intelligence.

Cheryl was the one to knock us out of our tech bubble into the real, human world, when she asked Larry, "So, Larry, what's your story? How did you get into what you're currently doing?"

"Well," he began, "when my parents were killed, I got some life insurance money."

Scott interrupted. "Your parents were killed?!"

"Yeah. Murdered. Bludgeoned to death." Then he paused, angled his head down and shook it. "Terrible shame."

"Did they catch the murderer?" Scott asked.

"Nope. Never did. So I took the money and invested it. I've done pretty good financially, and don't really have to work, but I do anyway, because this interests me. Network security. Besides, it's fun to try to break into systems."

Cheryl said, "I'm sorry for your loss."

Larry slowly nodded his head. "Thank you."

Doug asked, "Do you do pen testing?" I didn't know much about penetration testing, but I knew it involved sneaking into buildings late at night, or so I thought. I wasn't sure I would want to do that. I might prefer to sit in an office in front of a computer and let the other people break in with flashlights and try to avoid security. No thank you.

"I've done a little physical pen testing, but I prefer network pen testing. It's different."

"Isn't there any overlap between the two?" asked Scott.

"Yes. For example, if I walked into your office and sat down on one of the chairs, waiting for an appointment, I would try plugging my laptop into the network plug that is right there."

"Do we actually have a network plug in the waiting room?"

"Yes."

"What kind of access does it get you?"

"It used to give you access to all the printers."

"That's not so bad."

"Except that one of your printers wasn't up to date on its firmware. There was a known vulnerability that let new firmware be installed that could attach a payload, such as a crafted PDF file that would run when someone scanned a document."

"Wow. Really?"

"Yup. But I patched it. Everything is good now. It's secure."

"Does that mean you're done your security audit?"

"Pretty much. I might stop by tomorrow morning one more time. But until then, I have a parting gift to present." This got our attention. Larry was going to give someone a present? He reached down onto the floor and lifted up a bag. For a brief moment I thought he was going to bring out a gun and start shooting, but I guess that was an indication that my nerves were still on edge. I might not like Larry very much, but I'm pretty sure he wouldn't put a bullet in me. Even so, I may have still jumped a little when he announced, "It's for Jeff!" He handed me a plastic bag.

"Ah, thanks," I said as I accepted the package. I reached in and pulled out a Rubik's Cube.

"It's the latest Gan," said Larry. "They make the best speed cubes."

"Cool. Thanks, Larry." Maybe this guy wasn't that bad after all. I tried turning each side. It was smooth, and the corner cutting was amazing.

"Consider it as condolences for your apartment, as well as a token of our friendship."

We briefly discussed cubing methods, such as CFOP, Roux, and Petrus, then we all started getting up to go back to work. On our way out of the building, the thought came to me, "Larry is pursuing a friendship with you. You also need to pursue a friendship with someone," and Garth's picture came to mind. I stopped walking and groaned.

"What's wrong?" asked Cheryl, who stopped beside me. The others kept going.

"I think I'm supposed to do something for Garth."

"Like what?"

I looked around and saw a stand selling drinks. "Maybe a Dr. Pepper. Garth likes those."

"Good. I think you should." Then she looked at the lineup and said, "Well, see you later."

"You too."

When I got in line, a man got in line behind me. He was wearing a navy blue hoodie and covered his head, and whenever I glanced around behind me, he looked away. And when I paid for the Dr. Pepper and walked away, the man didn't buy anything but instead followed me. I started running.

CHAPTER 10

1:24 PM

I sprinted hard across the outdoor plaza, under the giant canopy, then toward our own building, the Johnston Terminal. Just before the stairs, I glanced back, expecting the man to slide a knife between my shoulder blades at any minute. Instead, I saw nothing, which itself startled me just enough to make me lose my footing and stumble as I tried to take the stairs two at a time and failed. I twisted around in mid-air and landed on my backside, staring back into the plaza.

Blue Hoodie was standing directly under the canopy, staring at me. Then he did something I didn't expect. He slowly raised his hands, grabbed his hood, and lifted it back off his face. I immediately recognized him. When he saw that I recognized him, he put his hood back on, turned, and walked away.

It took me a few seconds to process this, and when I was done, I was forced to conclude that this man shouldn't be chasing me. I should be chasing him.

So I got off the ground and started toward him. He glanced back and saw me, then started jogging. So I started running. I chased him through the plaza, then around the back side of the Greek restaurant, the Chinese restaurant, and the British restaurant. At some point I yelled, "Wait!", and "Stop!", but he didn't stop.

On the other side of Fort Gibraltar Trail, he climbed a chain link fence and dropped down the other side, a few feet from the train tracks that once served as a hub of distribution for the entire continent, and still did to some extent.

I reached him, seconds later, and said through the fence, between breaths, "What?" "What are you doing?" "What's going on?" "And why are you wearing a hoodie?"

He took his hood off again, looking around. "I didn't want the security cameras to see me. They have eyes everywhere."

"Who does?"

"Vesuvius, I presume. My former boss, Yash Nagi, is in jail, so probably not him." This was his butler, whom we chased down a few days ago.

"You were looking for work," I said. "Did you find any?"

He shook his head. "Still looking. But I did find an old phone that used to belong to Mr. Nagi."

"Can I see it?"

He examined the ground and said, "Ah... I think I'm not ready to betray my boss that much yet."

"So then why did you come looking for me?"

He looked back up into my eyes. "Because they are planning a hit."

"A hit?"

"Yeah. They're going to kill some people."

"What?! Who?" I was going to add "Me?" but got scared that he would say Yes.

"Not you, if you're wondering."

"And how do you know this?"

"Chat groups. I guess they forgot to take Mr. Nagi off some chat groups when he got taken in."

"You need to take this to the police. I know a guy..."

He waved his hand at me. "I'm not going anywhere near any police with this. They'll get me for being an accessory."

"Then why are you telling me?"

He paused, looked at the horizon, then back to me, then shrugged. "Because I thought you might care. I thought you might do something."

I paused to consider those words, then nodded slightly. "I do. I will."

He seemed to relax, ever so slightly, as if a weight was lifted off his shoulders.

"Who are they?" I asked.

"One is a YouTuber named Smith MacNeil."

I was shocked. I had just watched him last night talk about cracking cryptography. Why would they want this guy taken out? Maybe his conspiracy theory is more than just a conspiracy. Maybe TK15 is actuall...

The butler interrupted my thoughts with more information. "The other is the CEO of FutureTech."

I've never heard of that company before, but I was sure to check them out.

He pointed at me. "If you go anywhere near the police with this information, you'll never see me again."

"But the police can help. They can protect these guys."

He shook his head. "Police investigate crimes; they don't prevent crimes."

"I'm not sure that's true..."

I heard a train start rumbling down the track toward us. "I have something for you," I said, as I reached into my back pocket and pulled out a crumpled envelope and handed it to him through the wire fence.

"What is this?" he asked as he received it and started opening it.

"It's ten thousand dollars in cash."

His eyes opened wide. "Why are you giving this to me? If you were paying me for information, it's too late. You already have it."

"Yeah. I'm not paying you for information."

"Then what?"

"I'm... I'm making friends."

"You're making friends? With money? By giving people cash?"

I shrugged. "Yes."

He pondered that, as if he had never considered that thought before, then responded with, "Huh."

The train was almost upon us. Just before it was, he jumped away from the fence, darted across the tracks, and waited for the train to separate us.

"Wait!" I said. "What if I need to contact you?" But it was too late. He probably didn't hear my question, and I certainly couldn't hear if he answered. I stood there for a minute for the full length of the train to pass. When it did, the man was nowhere to be seen, but out in the distance I thought I saw a gray Honda Civic driving away, the same kind of car we chased the other day.

As I walked back to work, the weight of what just happened started to weigh heavy on me. I had just agreed to save the lives of two people who were being targeted by an evil man who may not even exist. How in the world was I supposed to do this? It's impossible! I can barely save myself, let alone people I don't know and have never met.

In my anguish, I cried out in my heart to God, and then tried to still myself enough to hear an answer. Two thoughts came to me. The first one was, "Yes, you have indeed been given a weighty responsibility." The second was, "But you have also been given help." I thought of Scott, Doug and Cheryl and felt slightly better. Maybe, just maybe, the four of us might be able to do something.

2:01 PM

As I entered our room, I saw the three guys working at

their desks. I would have made a general announcement if it wasn't for Garth there, who it seemed had rejected God's email address and wanted nothing to do with any of this. So I was hesitant to say what I had to say.

But as I was standing there, Garth's large form swiveled around in his chair and announced, "It appears as though Mr. Davis has an announcement for us, gentlemen." When I stood there, at a loss for words, he continued. "Very well, Jeff, go ahead. We are listening."

"Um... ah..." I hesitated, but when I saw Scott and Doug looking at me as if I had something important or ominous to report, I had to say it. "I just talked with Yash Nagi's butler." This caused eyebrows to rise all over the room.

"Yeah?" prompted Scott.

"And he said that he was on his boss's phone, and found out that there are two more people on the list to be... killed."

Silence.

It occurred to me then that they were probably expecting the next person after me to be them. I could tell they suddenly looked scared, but as I was about to remove their fears, Doug spoke out, rather courageously and asked, "Who is it?" I didn't know he had such strength in him. Maybe there was more to this guy than I knew about.

"Oh, it's not anyone here," I said. This caused everyone to relax slightly. Scott rubbed the back of his neck. "One guy is the YouTuber Smith MacNeil."

"What!?" exclaimed Scott. "Why?!"

I shrugged. "I don't know. And the other is the CEO of FutureTech."

"FutureTech? That's a dumb name for a company," said Scott.

"It might be, but their CEO is in trouble."

"Did this butler let slip who is planning to do the deed?" asked Garth.

I shook my head, but then added, "I guess Vesuvius."

"Who's that?" asked Doug.

"Some say he's the boss of Yash Nagi and Jade."

"The final boss, eh?" said Scott. "If we take him down, we all win. That's how it works in the video games."

"In the video games you get more than one life," I said. "I'm pretty sure we only get one. And nobody knows if this guy even exists. Apparently, if he does exist, he's pretty illusive."

"Well, we have to tell the police anyway."

"About that... the butler, um... his name is... James, I think. James told me to not go to the police, and I've thought about it, and I think we don't have to."

"People's lives are at stake," said Scott.

"I know. That's why we will warn them."

"How?"

"We do research on the Internet and track them down, and let them know. I promised James I would do something about this, and I'm going to. Now who wants to help me?"

"Of course I will, buddy," said Scott. "That's what we're here for."

"I'll help too," said Doug.

"I suppose if we're all going to participate, I may as well join you," said Garth. "I'm sure you could use my Internet searching prowess, especially considering lives are at stake, and considering the fact that our boss is not going to be in the rest of the day."

I smiled. "Thanks, everybody."

"Let's get to work, people," said Scott. "We have lives to save."

2:13 PM

And so we started researching.

Tracking down the CEO of FutureTech was the easy part.

It was a matter of public record. It wasn't a publicly traded corporation, but their website didn't mind showing off their top guy. His name was Robert Leland Alexander. In the picture, he stood tall in front of the FutureTech building behind him, his dark hair blowing in the breeze, his blue eyes looking out toward new horizons, as if by this man's charisma alone the future would come to them, thus making all their investors rich beyond anyone's wildest dreams.

And then we found all their contact details—physical address, email, online contact form, and phone number. I sent them an email with as much information as I could. I also sent the same thing in their online form. I feared it would be ignored. I should probably call them.

"Who wants to call FutureTech?" I asked the room.

"I'll do it," said Scott.

We had a shared document that we all added information to, and Scott found the phone number there. He activated his speaker phone so we could hear. The conversation went like this.

A woman's voice said, "Hello. FutureTech. How may I help you?"

Scott said, "Hey. Can I speak with Robert Alexander?"

"Who's calling?"

"This is Scott Stark. I'm calling from Omniscient Technologies."

"I'll forward you to our VP of Technologies, Kevin Polinsky."

"No! No. I need to speak with Robert himself."

"Would you like to speak with the executive CEO, Ryan Peters?"

"No. This isn't about technology... or business."

"A personal matter? Does Mr Alexander know you?"

"Uh... no, but it's important that I speak with him."

"Mr. Alexander is very busy, and a lot of people want to

speak with him..."

"Wait! Uh... Actually, yeah, we... we went to High School together. We're good buddies."

There was a very brief pause, then the woman said, "Thanks for calling Future Tech. Have a good day."

"Wait! Robert's going to die!"

There was another pause, in which case we thought we may have gotten through, then she said, "Don't call back, or I'll call the police." Then there was a click.

Wow. That didn't go well. Garth was the first to comment. "Do I even need to comment on how much of an astounding failure that phone call was?"

"Yeah, that wasn't good," said Scott.

"Now what do we do?" I said as I looked around.

"I'll do it," said Doug. I looked at him, not expecting him to do anything, since he normally doesn't ever do anything interesting.

"Really?" I said.

He slowly nodded. "Someone's life is in danger. I'm going to do everything I can." He shrugged. "And I can make a phone call."

"OK... thanks," I said.

He took out his own phone, punched the numbers, and also placed it in speakerphone mode. Soon the same woman answered.

"Hello. FutureTech. How may I help you?"

"Good afternoon. My name is Doug Grimm."

"What can I do for you?"

"I'm sorry to inform you of this, but we have reason to believe that your CEO, Robert Alexander, may be the target of an assassination plot."

There was silence again, then she said, "Are you the police?"

"No. I'm a concerned citizen."

"If this is true, I think we need to be talking with the police."

"Our informant left us strict instructions that we were not to go to the authorities. However, there is no reason you can't. Perhaps you should."

"OK. OK. What to do? I'll pass on your message to Mr. Alexander. He can make that call himself. Do you have any more details I can pass on to him?"

"I think so. We believe the threat is coming from a man known as Vesuvius."

"Vesuvius? OK. Anything else?"

"Not at this time, no. I realize it's not much to go on, but we have to take precautions. I hope you do what you have to do to stay safe."

"Yes. Of course. Thank you. Mr. Alexander is not in right now, but I will certainly give him this message. And I may call the police myself."

"Good. Thank you. I don't think there is anything else we can do right now, so I hope it all works out for you."

"Thank you."

"Bye"

"Bye"

Doug put his phone back into his pocket.

Garth commented again. "It never ceases to amaze me how much more talent one man in this office can have than another. I believe that phone call may have done the trick."

"I hope so," I said. "Yeah, Doug. That was very good."

"Amazing!" said Scott.

"I hope it will go just as well for Smith MacNeil."

2:48 PM

Tracking down Smith MacNeil was very different. There was no public record of him. All we could find of him was his

YouTube channel, and sending a YouTuber a message was so simple it was all over in five minutes.

So we sat around until Doug got an email from god@heaven. It said simply, "Don't give up. Track him down. Keep going. Hunt down the clues."

When he read it out loud to us, I took a peak at Garth, wondering what he thought of the idea of receiving an email from God. Would he despise the idea and berate us all? Or would he be open to the concept? But his face was a wall of granite.

"What?!" said Scott. "What else can we do? We have no idea of anything else."

"The email talked about clues," said Doug.

"Hidden where?" I asked. "In his YouTube videos?"

Nobody said anything as we all processed this idea. Did Smith somehow let slip where he lived? The one video I watched was of him in Scotland, but maybe he was just on vacation or something.

"Right!" declared Scott. "Smith has uploaded thirty-eight videos. That's about ten for each of us. We may as well start watching them as soon as possible."

"I'll take the earliest ten," said Doug.

"I suppose I will peruse and report on the next ten," said Garth.

"I'll get the third batch," said Scott.

"And I'll do the rest," I said "Thanks everyone. Hopefully we'll be able to find this guy and warn him. And... let's report on anything we find in our shared document. And... I'll go get us some coffee."

I brought coffee for everyone, and I brought Garth a Dr Pepper, who actually said "Thank you" to me. Then we donned our earphones and ear buds, sat back, and started watching YouTube to save this man's life.

A half hour later Doug said, "I think I might have

something."

"What is it?" asked Scott.

"In this video, Smith said he had to wake up early to watch the 7:16 AM launch of the latest SpaceX rocket."

"That's not much of a clue," I said.

"Jeff, Jeff, Jeff," began Garth. "I am in constant surprise at your naivete. A 7:16 AM launch tells us half of what we need to know. All we need to do is find a launch prior to when that video was uploaded, that was scheduled for the thirty-seventh minute of the hour, then look at the hour, and we immediately know his time zone. Half our work is done."

"That's brilliant, Garth," said Scott.

"Thank you, sir. Now when was the video uploaded, Doug?"

"Um... March 17."

"We know what we're looking for, gentlemen," said Garth. "Find us that launch."

We got back to it, and it was I who found it first. Soon I announced, "SpaceX launched a pile of satellites on March 18, 12:16 UTC... Wow."

Doug said, "Wow."

Garth said, "Indeed."

Scott said, "I don't get it."

I replied. "That's our time zone."

"Oh. Oh! Oh!! Smith might be here!"

"Statistically unlikely," said Garth. "His latitude still eludes us."

"Then let's get back to it," I said. "We still have more clues to find. We need to find his latitude."

We turned around and continued watching and skimming more YouTube videos by Smith MacNeil. Some of us recorded largely useless information in our shared document, like a video of his dog in his front yard, but at least it was something. I had finished watching most of my videos when Scott said, "I don't know if this is a clue. Smith just looked at his phone and announced the time."

We all looked over his shoulder to watch the video.

Garth said, "If there is a good shot of a shadow from which we could calculate its angle, we've got him." We watched a few scenes very closely, but we didn't see any shadows.

We turned back to our own computers, when Scott said that was his last video. It looked like we were going to come to a dead end, when Doug said simply, "I've got it. He was doing a video on astronomy and said that the angle of elevation to Polaris was 49.79 degrees."

"Huzzah, gentlemen!" announced Garth. "We've got him."

"Wow. You did that math fast," said Scott.

"No need for any math this time, my friend. He's right here."

"In the city?" I asked.

"Affirmative, assuming these two pieces of information are still current."

"So, even if he's here in the city," I started, "we still don't have his address."

"Maybe that video of his front yard showed his house number," Scott suggested.

"It did, but it was blurry," said Doug. "I couldn't read it."

"A Blind Deconvolution Algorithm may fix that," suggested Garth, as he turned back to his computer, and started doing math on pixels.

"Well, is there anything else for the rest of us to do?" I asked.

"The number of degrees was so specific," said Doug, "that it might be worth our time to go through that latitude, looking on Google Maps for his front yard."

"OK," I said.

"Let's do it!" said Scott.

So the three of us also got back to our computers and

started scanning streets in our city, looking for Smith's front yard. A few minutes later Scott called out, "I found it!!! Firbridge Crescent!", and showed us the same yard that was featured on Smith MacNeil's video. The shot also showed the number beside his front door. It was 125.

"I'd call it a tie," announced Garth, who also displayed a blurry but barely readable "125" on his screen.

"Wow, everyone," I said. "That was amazing. Thanks so much for helping." I looked at the time, then continued. "Shall we go for a drive?"

CHAPTER 11

4:50 PM

"Why, oh, why didn't we take my Mustang?!" Scott moaned for the second time from the back seat of Garth's gray Toyota Corolla. I was back there with him and it was a little cramped. Doug sat up front with Garth who was driving of course.

We were heading down Route 42, just crossing Midtown Bridge over the Assiniboine River.

"To repeat myself," began Garth, "We are taking my vehicle because it was parked closer, and we didn't feel up to trekking out to where you parked yours."

Scott replied, "And I said I don't like parking where it's so close to everyone else. My paint will get scratched by a bad driver."

Garth said, "Now if that isn't the most ironic thing spoken today—you accusing me of being a bad driver. Why don't you tell us then, Scott Stark, how many people you've struck with a vehicle in the last year?"

"Two that I know of," offered Doug.

"Hey! I was saving Jeff's life. Jade and Max were going to kill him on the Provencher Bridge."

"I'm very thankful for that, by the way," I added. "He did save my life."

"See? I saved Jeff's life."

"Well in this vehicle," continued Garth, "we drive safely and legally, which means we don't drive into people, or any other stationary objects, and we certainly don't do car chases."

I glanced at the speedometer. We were going just under the speed limit.

Just then we heard Michael Jackson start singing, "Man in the Mirror." It was coming from beside me. Scott pulled out his phone and glanced at it.

I said, "Got an email from God?"

He frowned at me. "Michael Jackson doesn't announce emails from God."

"No?"

"No. He announces YouTubers who are going live."

"You can customize that notification sound?"

"I can."

I didn't know you could. Maybe Scott hacked something. Cool.

Then Scott announced, "Guess what! Our friend Smith MacNeil just started broadcasting live."

I raised my eyebrows. That was interesting. Garth said, "You may connect your phone to my car's infotainment system. You'll find a Bluetooth device labeled 'TAXI-1729'".

"Thanks Garth. I'll do it." Scott said. Then, as he tapped his screen, he mentioned, "TAXI-1729. Why that name? Why not call it 'Garth-Car' or 'Super-Corolla' or something?"

"It has a perfectly fine name, thank you," Garth replied. "It's a reference to the great mathematician Ramanujan"

"Or 'Carth'," I suggested.

"No," he replied.

"Maybe if it were Star Wars themed, he might like it," said Doug. "How about 'Toyodda'?"

"'Car-Car-Blinks'," suggested Scott, "or 'Bluebacca'."

I sat and smiled at their imagination, then Smith's voice boomed in the air around us, and in us, and both Scott and

Garth scrambled to turn the volume down.

The Scottish voice said, "I'm Smith MacNeil, and you're watching TechnoSomething, the show where I usually talk about something. In this episode, I won't be talk'n. I'll be do'n."

I glanced at Scott who was happily staring at his phone. I said, "Did you want to share that screen?"

"Oh!" he announced. "Smith is just at his desk. Nothing to see."

The voice continued. "You see, I just got my hands on this 3D holographic projector. It's a few years old now, but still going strong. Let me show you how it works."

I stared out the car's window as I listened to Smith MacNeil drone on about his holographic projector. I watched department stores come into view, and move off out of view, to be replaced by parking lots, restaurants, and a church or two. One of those churches I recognized. It was a rainy night when I visited it, hoping to find out how to hear from God when he stopped emailing me. I was very disappointed that day, but today was much different. Today, I have learned the technique of hearing from God, and I was in a vehicle of friends, and it was a cheerful and sunny day. Life was good.

As Garth turned a corner, onto a residential street, the sound of a gunshot cracked out over the sound of everything else. We all looked around in every direction, hoping to see something we should flee from, but there was nothing dangerous out there.

Smith MacNeil's voice went silent. For a moment I thought the gunshot took out our entertainment system, but then I clued into what was going on. The gunshot, of course, was in the YouTube video. Smith was no longer speaking.

"Share your screen, Stark!" yelled Garth from the driver's seat. "What's going on?"

"Nothing," said Scott. "Smith just stopped speaking. Now he's looking up past the camera."

His voice now continued, but as the YouTuber Smith MacNeil, but as a Scottish man not happy about being interrupted. "Oy! I'm recording here! Don't you know a film set when you see it?"

"He just walked out of the shot," Scott said.

There may have been some muffled voices. Then more gunshots. Then cries of pain. More gunshots. Then silence. Then a door closing. And after that, nothing.

5:14 PM

The four of us looked at each other, not knowing what to say.

Scott began. "What... just...happened..."

"Drive faster!" I shouted. If Smith was in trouble, we needed to get there ASAP.

"I'm beginning to have second thoughts about this mission," said Garth, who looked a little worried.

"We're soon there," said Doug. "His house should be just up ahead on the left." He pointed.

I followed the direction of his finger and found, parked on the road, a vehicle that looked familiar. It was a light blue Dodge Charger. I recognized it as the one that almost drove into me when I was chasing down the person who bombed my apartment. "Hey! That's them!" I shouted, as I pointed to the vehicle, which appeared empty at the moment. "That's who blew up my apartment!"

Garth hammered the car to a stop, presumably so I could get out. But instead, he started backing up. Then he turned the wheel, circled the car around, and sped away at top speed.

"Stop! Stop the car!" I yelled. "We need to go check on Smith MacNeil!"

"No, Jeff!" said Garth. "We do not need to go check on Smith MacNeil. We need to save our lives. We need to move our physical bodies away from the people who would kill us. That's what we need to do. And we need to do this with haste."

I noticed he was speeding. So much for being a safe driver. He was a cowardly driver, is what he was. I considered jumping out, but we were traveling far too fast.

So instead I took out my phone and called 911.

The female voice said, "911. What is your emergency?"

Now it may have been Garth's erratic driving, or the fact that we just witnessed a murder, but for some reason I wasn't thinking quite as sharply as I could have. I said, "Uh... hi... I... we... I think we just may have witnessed a murder."

"What is your location?"

"We're on... Doug! Where are we?"

He said, "Turning back onto Route 42 North."

I said into my phone, "42 North"

She said, "And what did you see?"

"Um... nothing exactly, but we heard shots."

"Gunfire?"

"Yes."

"Where exactly did you hear it?"

"We think it came from 125 Firbridge Crescent."

"Where were you when you heard it?"

"Oh, we were a few blocks away, but we're sure it came from 125 Firbridge Crescent."

"How do you know it came from there?"

"Well... we..." It just occurred to me that this wasn't going to sound good. "You see, we did some math, tracking down this YouTuber."

There was a brief pause, then she said, "Go on."

"So we found his address using SpaceX and the declination of Polaris."

More silence, then, "But you heard gunfire."

"Yes! Yes we did."

"What was your location when you heard it?"

"We just turned off the 42... onto..."

Doug said, "Onto Bairdmore Boulevard."

I continued, "Bairdmore Boulevard."

"And it sounded like the gunshots came from 125 Firbridge Crescent? That's pretty specific."

"Oh, well, we actually heard the shots over our car speakers, not from outside. We were listening to the YouTube video."

The voice started sounding almost upset now. "So you were listening to a video in your car, and the gunshots were actually part of the video."

"Well, yes..."

"So you didn't hear any gunshots in real life?"

"Uh... no... no, I don't think so."

"OK, so let me get this straight. You were listening to a YouTube video in your car, and you heard gunshots in the video, and you think they came from 125 Firbridge, because of SpaceX and the declination of Polaris. Is that right?"

I was a little taken aback at the accuracy of what she just said, so I just said, "Yes. And we saw a light blue Dodge Charger."

She said, "I will send an officer to check on 125 Firbridge Crescent."

"Thank you."

"You're welcome. Thank you for calling 911. Goodbye." The call ended.

I began to feel frustrated, too. "Agh. Can we turn around?"

Garth said, "Not on your life, buddy."

I sat and frowned. Maybe I should jump out. Maybe the 911 operator was right. This story did sound incredible. Maybe the Dodge Charger was not actually Veronica's. It may have been a coincidence. I'll just go check on Smith myself when I get my car."

My phone, still in my hand, vibrated. I just got a text

message from Cheryl. It said, "Be at Mom and Dad's at 6:00," followed by a kiss emoji. What?! Then I remembered that she had invited me over for this evening. Hmm... six o'clock is in just over half an hour. When we get back to the parking lot at the forks, I'll just barely have time to get there for six. "Agh," again! So much for Smith MacNeil. I'm sure the visit from the police officer will do everything I could, anyway.

6:02 PM

I let my eyes land on the Audis and Porsches and other exotic cars filling the driveways of Kingston Crescent, and wondered if I would ever be this rich. I concluded I probably wouldn't, because I was working by the hour, and these people owned whole businesses and had investments. Cheryl's father was one of them. He owned Omniscient, or at least some of it. I've never seen him at the office, because he doesn't run it at all. The CEO, Peter Steele, runs the business. My boss, Nigel Merywether, reports to Peter. I don't know how Peter became the CEO. Maybe Cheryl's dad might know. Maybe I should ask him one day.

I turned into their driveway, which was full, and parked my Honda Civic as out of the way as I could. There was a vehicle I didn't recognize. It was a silver BMW SUV.

I rang the doorbell and Cheryl's little brother, Tim, answered it. "Hey Jeff," he said. "Do you like my new BMW?"

"Um... yeah. Is that yours?"

"I wish. Dad has a friend over."

"OK."

Cheryl came in and gave me a kiss of greeting.

"Ugh," said Tim. "Go do your thing elsewhere."

"You're just jealous," said Cheryl. "Get yourself a girlfriend like a normal young man."

"I tried. I can't find anyone worthy of me."

As we walked farther into the house, Tim continued. "Well, there was that senator's daughter, but when she ran off with that astronaut, I swore off love for good."

"I'm going to help Mom in the kitchen," said Cheryl.

"Even when I met Miss Norway at that pool party," continued Tim, "She was really into me, but I had to let her down. Poor thing."

I looked over and saw Cheryl's dad, Daryl, in the living room, sitting with another man I'd never met. Daryl waved us over.

"I broke her heart that day, as I've done with a lot of women. That's just my lot in life, now. I may as well accept it."

The men were seated in armchairs. Tim handed the visitor a piece of paper, which he signed, then Daryl signed it too and pocketed it. As I sat on one end of a brown leather sofa, Tim sat on the other and said to me, "They just agreed to do some pen testing on each other."

I knew what penetration testing was. It's when you test the security of someone's network by trying to hack into it. But I was just unsure about what was just agreed upon. Was someone going to try to hack our network? That didn't seem like fun. Or maybe Larry's work was about to be put to the test. But before I got a chance to ask, Daryl introduced me.

"That is Jeff," he said, pointing to me, "my daughter Cheryl's boyfriend."

I said, "Hi" to the man. He was bald, but smiling and happy.

Tim said to the man, "And of course you know me. I just printed out your agreement, or perhaps 'our' agreement. I'll be taking over the family business soon, so we may as well begin our professional relationship."

"Not so hasty, son," said Daryl. "Bob is just a friend from University. We don't really have a professional relationship."

Tim shrugged.

Sometimes I thought he was actually serious, trying to weasel his way into his dad's businesses, but most of the time I just ignored him for his outlandish ways. You never know with that guy.

"Do you remember in University," Daryl began, "when we found that empty broom closet?"

"Of course I remember," said Bob. " We studied there, and ate there, and hid from the authorities there. We called it our bastion."

"Yes! Bastion. I remember that name. And it had a network cable running through it, and we tried to hack into the network."

"It didn't work."

"No, it didn't. Shortly after that, they found our closet and locked it for good."

"Probably because we messed with the cable. Actually, you're the one who did it, Daryl, not me."

"I did, but it was your idea, Bob. You always got me into trouble."

"Ah, good times."

"That was the height of my IT career," Daryl said. "I found better success leading a team of smart people, rather than being smart myself."

"Yes. Same with me. But I continued to CEO while you went into buying companies. You should try running a company, Daryl. It's fun. It keeps you young."

"Peter is doing a fine job at Omniscient. He doesn't need my help."

Just then Cheryl came, and called us to the table, so we got up, and made our way there. On the way, I noticed Bob was not quite as tall, and not quite as lean as Daryl was. He would make a good Santa Clause, if Santa was bald.

"I'm looking forward to talking with you, Jeff," said Bob to me. "I've read about you in the news."

I gulped.

6:43 PM

Through mouthfuls of lasagna, I explained to Bob about my dad and Yash Nagi. When I was done, Bob asked me, "Is it true Jade and Yash worked together?"

I nodded. "Well, at least they knew each other."

He asked another question. "Is it true they both reported to the same man?"

I looked at him to try to find out what he was getting at. How much did this man know? I nodded. When he didn't immediately reply, I started getting nervous. What was he getting at? What did he know? Who was this man, anyway? He wasn't... The blood drained from my face as it dawned on me who he really was. Was he the one we were looking for? Was he the one who was actually looking for me, trying to kill me? And now he has me trapped in this house, and he's going to kill not just me, but this whole family as well. I froze, trying desperately to think of what to do. Run, or fight, or something.

But then he smiled warmly and said, "Relax Jeff. I'm not Vesuvius, let me assure you. In fact, I'm also trying to find him. I've been trying to find him for some time now."

My breathing returned to normal, and Cheryl put her hand on my leg, since she saw that I was distraught.

I said, "I... we... have been trying to find him..." I shook my head. "But we can't. He's... hard to find."

"Yes, he is. And he's not normal—probably a psychopath." Cheryl's hand squeezed my leg harder. I put my hand on top of hers, to comfort her.

"He's like the joker, huh?" said Tim. "And Jeff is Batman. I guess that makes me Robin."

"You're crazy," said Cheryl.

"Whatever you say, Batgirl."

Bob said, "We should get together and compare notes."

I started nodding, but was interrupted by the song "La Cucaracha." I looked around the table, wondering who would have that song as a ringtone. It was Bob. His face grew serious as he listened to the caller. He mumbled some reply or something, then hung up and stared at nothing at all in the middle of the table.

"What is it, Alex?" Daryl asked his friend.

He sighed, then tried unsuccessfully to put a smile back on his face. "My company was just bought out. I have to go meet the new owner."

"What?!" exclaimed Daryl. "Just like that?"

"Apparently." He stood. "Daryl, it was good meeting again, and your family. Take care of yourselves. And I apologize for the abruptness, but I have to go. Have yourselves a good evening. Until next time." He started walking toward the door.

Daryl got up to follow him.

I sat there, staring at the last two bites of lasagna on my plate, trying to understand a feeling in my gut. It wasn't physical; my stomach was fine. Maybe I was nervous about these two men talking about the company I worked for, because it would most likely involve me in some way. Probably. I did feel anxious, but that wasn't anything special. Maybe I was worried about this Bob, and what he could tell me about Vesuvius. That must be it. My brain was just moving too fast. I just needed to relax, that's it. I closed my eyes, and tried to picture God standing next to me. When I did that, I expected him to be smiling, and loving, and caring. He was, of course, but he was also staring at me like I should be doing something important.

I imagined asking him, "What? What?" He motioned for me to follow the two men outside, but that didn't make any sense.

I should have simply obeyed that feeling, but instead I

opened my eyes, and picked at the pasta on my plate with a fork. The forkful of noodles and cheese and sauce were halfway to my mouth when I paused and said, "Cheryl, why did your dad call Bob 'Alex'?"

Her mom answered. "It's his last name, dear. Alexander."

My fork twitched. Then my whole arm started shaking. Then tremors progressed to the rest of my body before I could speak out loud, but when I did, I said, or almost yelled, "Bob Alexander? As in Robert Alexander!? As in the CEO of FutureTech?!" As in the second person destined to die today!?

She said, "Yes. Why?"

As I fought my chair to get up as fast as possible, my brain filled in the missing pieces. The picture on the website was when he was younger, and had more hair, or was wearing a wig. The camera was held low, so he looked taller. But now that I see it, it was the same guy. In a panic, I bolted for the door, shouting "Wait! Wait!"

When I got to the door and opened it, Robert Alexander was backing his silver SUV down the driveway, and Daryl was on his way back inside. The explosion lifted Daryl nearly off his feet, and tossed him like a rag doll onto the concrete. I was also pushed back into the house against a wall and the floor. I may have hit my head and blacked out for a second; I don't remember. But when I got up and looked at the damage, the SUV was a smoldering wreck. The driver's door was missing, and I could see his body inside. Eyes open, seeing nothing, his skin that was once white was now red and black. Blood was everywhere, including running out of several places on his lifeless body. I didn't go near. I didn't have to.

In a daze, I turned to Daryl. He was on his front, unmoving, so I rolled him over. His face was scraped up. I tried to feel for a pulse by his neck, and I thought I felt one, a weak one. He must still be alive.

By then the women were outside, also in a panic. I stood

up, and let them hover over their father and husband, willing and pleading for him to stay alive. I saw Tim, and told him to call 911. He nodded.

Suddenly I felt very weak, so I walked over to the house. After emptying my stomach behind the bushes, I sat on the ground, resting against the siding.

I had been warned this very day of two murder attempts, hoping I could do something to save these people. I had botched them both.

CHAPTER 12

8:40 PM

"He is in a coma. We have him on anti-seizure drugs and diuretics," the doctor explained to us as we sat in the waiting room.

Cheryl leaned against me in the chair next to mine. Tim and Cheryl's mom were on the other side of her.

"What are the diuretics for?" asked Tim.

"They reduce the fluid in the tissue, thus reducing pressure inside the brain," he replied. "It is not an induced coma, so he may wake up at any time."

Cheryl's mom asked, "So he's going to be alright?"

"The important things we're looking out for right now are inflammation, bleeding, or reduced oxygen supply to the brain. So far we see none of these."

She seemed to relax a little. "So he's going to be alright?"

"It's too early to make a prediction, but I've seen worse. It might go downhill, or he might wake up tomorrow."

"We'll pray he wakes up."

"Do you have any more questions?"

"Can I see him?"

"Yes. We allow two visitors at a time. And of course he won't respond to you."

I spoke quietly to Cheryl, "Do you want to see him?"

She shook her head. "Take me home."

I announced, "You two can go see him. I'll take Cheryl home. Keep us up-to-date on anything."

"We will. Thanks, Jeff."

Cheryl's mom and Tim got up to go with the doctor. Cheryl and I left the room, and the hospital, and climbed into my car.

As I was driving, I said, "He'll be OK."

She replied, "I hope so. The doctor said he might wake up tomorrow." After a minute, she asked, "How do you feel about it in your spirit? Do you hear God saying anything?"

I paused, trying to relax, then I said, "I feel his big strong arms around me right here." I patted my chest.

"Yeah. Me too. I don't know what it means, but it feels good."

"Yeah."

We didn't talk much on the way to her house. When we arrived, I walked her to the door, and gave her a good-night kiss.

"Are you coming in?" she asked.

I shook my head. "This afternoon we tried to rescue a YouTuber from... from... from experiencing a similar fate, probably also from Vesuvius. I want to visit the scene of the crime."

She frowned and said, "Why?!", as if she couldn't understand why I would want more of this.

I shrugged. "I was personally warned about these people, and we left the YouTuber's place before we knew exactly what happened. I want to see if there is anything I can see."

"Be careful, Jeff."

I nodded. "I will be." Then I gave her another kiss and a hug, and walked away. Maybe I'll find answers at 125 Firbridge Crescent.

_9:33 PM_

I parked my Civic half a block from 125 Firbridge Crescent, among the other vehicles parked in front of their homes. It was an old part of town, and the trees were large, but they still let in enough light at this time of the evening for me to scan for any suspicious-looking vehicles. I didn't see any, especially any light blue Dodge Chargers—or anything else suspicious, either, which was mostly black vans and black BMWs, in my case.

I decided to do a drive-by. I pulled out into the road, and slowly made my way between the cars, keeping an eye on 125, and the other eye on the road, in case someone came at me from the front.

As I approached the house in question, it looked completely normal. It had a gray roof, faded white siding, some grass, and all the lights were off.

Just then a vehicle bore down on me from the front with its lights on. It was black, which made it suspicious, but it was only a Mini, which couldn't be suspicious if it tried. It passed me, and I watched it go in my rear-view mirror.

By then I was past the house, so I decided to circle the block and try again.

On my second attempt, I parked near 125, and turned off the car. I sat low in my seat and stared at the building for a good ten minutes. Absolutely nothing happened.

I took a good look at the front door, seeing if I could make out any signs of forced entry. I couldn't see any. And there wasn't any police tape either. It just looked like a normal house with its lights off.

My thoughts were all over the place. On one hand, we may have got the location wrong and somebody else lives here. On the other hand, there might be a dead body inside, and the building will blow up in my face if I approach it. Or maybe Smith MacNeil pulled out his own gun and chased the intruders out. Na, now my mind was just wandering.

Two things made me go knock on the door. The first was that if someone was inside who needed help, and I could help, I wouldn't be able to live with myself if I did nothing. Somebody had to do something. And the second, was that I wanted answers. I was tired of not knowing, tired of losing, tired of being the tail that got wagged, instead of the one doing the wagging. So I decided to wag.

It might kill me, but the decision had been made. I got out of the car, closed the door behind me, and started walking. A car passed by me on the street, but I didn't stop. Oh, it made me nervous, yes, but I didn't stop. I walked all the way to the door, paused, then knocked.

Nothing happened. Nobody came to the door. I knocked again. Still nothing. So I looked in the front window. It looked like a house to me—no dead bodies on the floor, no blood, no bullet casings.

I decided to close my eyes, and imagine God next to me. I stilled my mind and my heart, and whispered the question, "What should I do?"

The thought came to me, "You're tired, Jeff. You need to get some rest."

I opened my eyes, and admitted the idea was probably right. I was tired. It had been another long day.

Friday, 8:03 AM

I spent the night at Scott's again, on his sofa, which was not comfortable. And now I was looking forward to a good-morning hug and kiss from my girlfriend. It's too bad we meet in an office setting. Maybe we should meet out in a hallway or something.

As I rounded the corner to her cubicle, I found myself smiling at the back of her red hair and started saying, "Good mor...," but Scott interrupted me.

He grabbed both my shoulders, turned me toward him, and declared, "We have a problem. It's huge. It's a huge problem. You have to help us."

Of course I was concerned. "What's wrong?"

"It's God's email address. It..." But before he finished, we were interrupted again by the big boss himself, Peter Steele, from his nearby office.

"Jeffrey," he said. "I would like to speak with you in my office please."

I turned from my friend to go to his room.

"And Cheryl too, please," he added.

I poked my head back into her cubicle and said, "Cheryl..."

"I heard," she said. "I'm coming."

As the two of us walked the twenty feet to the boss's office, I planned to grab her hand and whisper something to her, and as Peter stepped into his office to wait for us, I started to make my move. Just as I brushed her hand with mine, Scott piped up from right behind us, "Come talk to me as soon as you're done in there. It's crazy."

I sighed. "OK." Then we entered Peter's office and sat down.

He closed his door behind us, and then sat back into his own chair on the other side of the desk.

He paused a moment, looking at us, then began. "I heard, Cheryl, that your father had an accident yesterday."

She nodded. "He's in a coma, but I'm hoping he's going to make a full recovery." Now that I got a good look at her face, I noticed her eyes were puffy and red, and looked like she didn't get a lot of rest. My heart broke for her. I longed to hold her tightly and console her.

Peter continued. "There are a number of things we need to discuss. Firstly, I'm sorry, Cheryl, for this difficult time you and your mother must be going through. I pray you have strength to endure it. I also hope, as do we all, that Daryl makes a full and complete recovery."

"Thank you," she said.

"The next thing I need to decide is what to tell the staff. They may hear about this in the news, but I think it's best if we... if I tell them first. So in order for me to accurately say what happened, it would help if you told me yourself what happened." He waited, his gaze fixed on Cheryl.

Cheryl turned to look at me, so I said to Peter, "I was there yesterday evening. I saw the whole thing."

"Were you? I had you in here because I knew you and Cheryl were dating, but I didn't know you were there personally."

"I was. I was at their place for supper."

"In that case, would you tell me what happened?"

I paused, not just wondering how to put events into words, but also wondering how much to say. Should I just talk about Daryl? What about Robert Alexander? What about the fact that he was also looking for Vesuvius? What about the fact that there was a credible threat on his life? And I couldn't save him. What about the butler? What about Smith MacNeil?

I searched for some words to use to report what happened, and found myself saying these. "Robert Alexander left during supper, and Daryl went to see him to his car. Then I followed them out. Then Robert's car blew up... killing him. And the blast threw Daryl to the ground. And me. But I got up, but he didn't. And now he's in a coma."

Peter took a deep breath and let it out. "You witnessed it?"

"Yes."

"Very well. I will send an email to the staff. Thank you, Jeff. And now, concerning the press, we should try to downplay these events as much as possible, if we are approached. We don't want to give any impression that Omniscient is in any way not fully functional, because it is. I am here. Nigel is here. All our developers are here. It is business as usual. Agreed?"

I nodded. Cheryl nodded.

"And now the final topic I want to address is this. Since we are trying to convey to the press that everything is business as usual, it would be beneficial to the company for both of you to continue to come in every day. This is just for the sake of optics, of course. However, that being said, if the stress of what's going on is too much to take, you may relax your work hours. I don't want to push you more than you can handle."

Cheryl nodded. I said, "OK."

Peter sat back in his chair and said, "All right. You are dismissed. Take care of yourselves."

As Cheryl and I left the room, I remembered that Scott had a problem.

8:32 AM

On my way to my desk, I glanced left at Garth's little whiteboard, expecting the joke of the day, but to my surprise it was blank. The whiteboard was all white. I looked right, and saw Doug, so I said, "The joke of the day is blank. Isn't Garth in today?"

Doug rotated his chair so he was facing me, a smile on his face that told of deep joy. He said, "Garth is in today."

A little confused, I replied, "But no joke?"

Doug continued to smile. "You should ask him about that."

I didn't feel like seeking out Garth, and talking with him, not if I could help it, so I shrugged, and sat down in front of my computer. But I could tell that Doug wasn't turning away.

He said again, "You'll probably be interested in what he has to say."

I glanced at him, then back at my screen. Yes, he may have made me curious, but not curious enough. Garth hasn't been a big source of happiness to me recently. I grabbed my cup, and said, "I'm going for coffee." Doug didn't reply.

On my way to the kitchen, I went past the server room, and as I did, the door opened and Larry came out. He smiled at me with that Larry kind of smile, which meant that he was simply pulling the correct muscles on his face. It wasn't the same time zone as Doug's deep joy. He said, "neighbor!" and walked with me.

He said, "Jeff, I'm done here, but I wanted to talk to you one last time." He stopped walking, and was about to speak, but then changed his mind, as if he didn't like the location. So he motioned me to walk with him. We walked around the kitchen corner, then down that far hallway until we almost reached the receptionist. Then he stopped and poked a finger at my chest. "Your problem, Jeff, is that you make emotional connections."

Ah, here was go again. This is the same thing he said to me in his car the other day on the way to my apartment.

"You let people get close to you," he continued. "This will be your downfall. This... love... this... compassion. It will be your downfall."

"But I got you this job. Isn't that a good thing?"

That made him pause, but then he smiled, and then started laughing. Not a happy laugh either. "Your compassion for me, your neighbor, made you get me this job. Jeff, you don't even know me. You think just because I live next to you, and pretend to be happy all the time that I'm a nice guy? Jeff, your compassion is a weakness. If I mess up this network, it was your fault, because you got me in here. Your niceness would be the downfall of the whole organization."

"But you're a professional."

He sneered and kept right on going. "And what about your girlfriend's dad? He was the friend of a guy who got killed. That's what happens when you make friends. You get caught up in their deaths. Your compassion, your kindness, your love... it will be your death, too."

He started to walk away, but then came back for more. "You said the other day in the car that we shouldn't act like the culture, that we shouldn't follow everyone else, and I believed you. That's why I... But I see now that you didn't mean turning your back on love, you meant embracing love. That's the opposite direction, Jeff. Love is what's going to get you killed, not saved. You'll see. You'll all see."

In my shock, I had no words. I just watched him turn and walk away, then to make my surprise even greater, his countenance changed from anger and rage to simple delight as he saw something in the reception area that made him happy. I heard him say, "Oh! A dog! I love dogs. Are you a good boy, good boy? Yes you are. Beautiful dog you have there."

8:40 AM

I couldn't help but wonder and ponder about Larry on my way for coffee. I didn't understand him at all. But did he say that he was done here? Maybe I wouldn't have to ponder him anymore, because he'll be gone. And if I never live in my apartment anymore, I guess I won't see him at home either. Part of me was relieved, but part of me felt like God had given me an assignment with Larry that I had failed. I didn't know what I could do about that now, so instead, I found the coffee maker, and poured myself a cup.

On my way back to my desk I happened to glance through the open door of the server room, and saw Garth. He was doing something I'd never seen him do before, and that really got my attention. He was sitting on a chair, with his eyes closed, head tilted up, and smiling a genuine, peaceful smile. It was so unlike him that I found myself staring. He looked so happy that I considered asking if he was OK.

Just when I decided that it was too weird, and I should

move on, he opened his eyes and saw me. Seeing as I just got caught in an awkward situation, I quickly started to go, but he called, "Jeff!"

I came back and he said, "Do you know why, Jeff Davis, that there is no comic posted this morning?"

"No."

"The reason is because today is not a day of joviality. It is a day of mourning. The whiteboard is white, just like a flag of surrender is white. I have surrendered, Jeff." He let his gaze wander far off. "I have surrendered. I fought hard, but in the end... I lost. I have lost everything, and I don't know who I am anymore."

This weirdness was almost enough to make me run away, but with the bit of curiosity I had, I asked, "What do you mean?"

He looked at me. "You're the one who gave me God's email address. That's what I mean. I tried it. It seemed to work, which is impossible. Utterly impossible. I tried everything... everything!"

I nodded. "I tried everything too."

"I even wrote my own email client. God still answered me. I added logging and debug statements in the code everywhere..." He shook his head. "God still answered me. It's impossible."

I nodded my head again.

He continued. "In the end I was forced to conclude that it was not actually possible. It was, in fact, impossible. I had been living in an impossible world. The world I thought existed—the one with known laws of physics—it doesn't exist. It probably never has. Maybe I've been wrong about God forever. I also know that me being wrong is impossible as well, but maybe that is true too." He paused. "And so I surrendered. I turned my face toward the impossible, and looked into his face. He met me, Jeff. I met with God."

I didn't really know how to reply to that, so I just said, "What... what was he like?"

Garth didn't answer right away. He sort of gazed into the distance, and then looked up as if searching for words, then scrunched his eyebrows as if disagreeing with the words that came, then finally concluded with "Love." He shrugged as if that was everything that needed saying. "It was as if liquid love was being poured over me. At first I resisted, but then I surrendered. I breathed it in. I let it define me. It is who I am now. I'm a different person, because of his love."

I said, "There wasn't any judgment?"

Garth laughed. "If there was, it was a sword I would have gladly swallowed. If he spoke any words against me, I would have welcomed them, because all his words are kind and gentle. He is welcome to say anything to me, do anything to me or with me. He is the only thing I desire."

Then Scott appeared, grabbed both my shoulders, looked me in the eyes and said, "Jeff. We have a problem, a big problem. God's email address stopped working."

CHAPTER 13

8:59 AM

I stood in the break room. Seated on the sofas in front of me were Scott, Garth, and Doug. As I started speaking, Cheryl walked in and said softly to me, "You know that dream I had of people following you?" She pointed to the floor. "This is it." Then she sat down, smiled, and looked at me.

I took a deep breath, and tried to let the stress out. Then I scratched the side of my head and said, "Uh... I guess the reason we're here is because we had God's email address, and it quit working." The guys nodded at me.

"Does it work for you?" Doug asked.

"No. Not anymore. Well, it did that once, or twice, but no, it quit working for me."

"What did you do?" Doug asked again.

"Well, I was riding on a bus..."

"I'll check the bus schedule," said Scott, pulling out his phone.

"It's not about the bus!" said Cheryl. "Let the man finish."

They all looked at me again, so I said, "Uh... I was riding on a bus, and there was a man there who explained to me how to hear from God. Apparently it was his job or something."

The guys stared back at me in confusion, but didn't say anything, so I continued. "I know, it sounds weird. Maybe God put him there in answer to my prayers." More staring, so I continued again. "So he gave me four steps on how to hear from God."

I stared at them, as if expecting them to take out a ringed notepad and chewed-up pencil, and start taking notes. None of them did, but finally Doug whipped out his phone and said, "Ready." The other three guys begrudgingly did the same.

"OK, the first step is to calm yourself down, because it's hard to hear from God in a bustling environment. So take some deep breaths or something, maybe some relaxing music. Maybe put a smile on your face."

"Coldplay helps me relax," said Scott.

"Adele," said Doug.

"John Williams," said Garth.

"Never heard of him," said Scott.

"Uncultured swine," replied Garth again, not even bothering to turn his head.

"So, moving on," I continued, "the music shouldn't have words, because they will interfere with hearing words from God. It should just get you into a relaxed, feely mood, instead of an analytical, thinking mood."

"So the opposite of what we do all the time every day," said Scott.

"Uh... maybe. OK, so that was the first one. Relax. The second step is to look for vision."

"I thought we were trying to hear from God," said Scott.

"Yes, well, it turns out that hearing is easier if you also look. So, instead of closing your eyes and not seeing anything, try closing your eyes and imagining God sitting next to you, or imagine yourself at a beach or something."

"In my car," said Scott with his eyes already closed.

"OK. Sure. Good."

"It's working."

"Um... you could tell us what you see."

"I'm sitting in my car, and God is next to me. He's wearing

white and smiling at me. He's just glad to be with me in my car. He's glad I invited him, as if he likes just hanging out with me, not doing anything."

"Good. I think you're doing it. Sounds good to me. So the first step is to relax, and the second is to look for vision. The third is to tune in to spontaneity."

"That one could use some elaboration," said Garth.

"Sure. For example, if you do math or anything in your head, one thought will follow another. But if God talks to you, a brand new thought will suddenly pop in there that didn't come from anywhere else in your head."

"I see. It's a spontaneous thought."

"Exactly. It suddenly just comes to rest on your mind. So, Scott, if you see God in your car, and his mouth is moving, and words are landing in your head, that could be him talking."

"'Could be'?" asked Scott.

I shrugged. "Yeah, I can't guarantee any of this stuff, but I think it probably is. But maybe not, because it's also possible to miss it."

The guys groaned. I continued. "So you have to test what you get."

"How?" asked Doug.

"Well, God's words are peaceful, uplifting, encouraging, healing. If you don't feel those, it's probably not from him."

"That makes sense."

"And the fourth step is to write it down."

"For those who don't have a stellar memory," said Garth.

"Yes, it is for remembering afterwards, but also, it's to stay in the mood, to stay in flow..."

"Stay in the zone?" suggested Garth.

"Yes. The zone," I said. "Because when you stop and think about if a word was from God or not, you leave the zone and you have to get back into it again. It's better to stay in the zone, and write down everything, then test it afterwards."

Garth said, "I would like to try this right now."

I said, "OK." The guys, and Cheryl too, closed their eyes, and soon were writing in their phones. I wandered over to the window and looked outside. A few stories down, standing on the ground looking up at me, was a man I'd seen two times in the last week. I turned to go toward the stairs, because I decided that I needed to see him again.

9:18 AM

When I exited the Johnston Terminal building through the back doors, I immediately saw James Kuff looking at me, as if expecting me to come find him. Doesn't he know that the chances of me accidentally seeing him out the window are really, really small? Come on, send an email or something.

I crossed the street and said, "Hi James," to him.

I nodded. "Jeff," then continued to look around, as if paranoid. I remembered I should probably be doing the same. He said, "Congratulations. I think you saved someone's life yesterday."

I stared at him, wondering what he was talking about. The two men I tried to save were both dead. But no, I only knew of Robert Alexander. "Smith MacNeil?" I asked.

He nodded again. "Did you like his little death-appearing act? And he did it live. Genius."

I was shocked. I stared at James, wondering if it was really true. Finally I said, "That was all an act? I heard that live. We listened to that as we were driving to his house."

James smirked. "From what I heard, the guys sent to take him out weren't very happy."

"Where is he now?"

He shook his head. "Haven't the foggiest idea. If he was smart, he would be a thousand miles from here. Maybe I should be, too."

I was tempted to agree with him, but then caught myself. "It's better to stay and see these guys come to justice."

James laughed out loud at that one. "Ha ha. You're funny, Jeff. That's what I like about you. You're so... naive."

"But you must have a lot of information on them, James. You should testify in court."

"Vesuvius would never let me live. I'll put effort into not dying, thanks. And staying out of jail at the same time. And paying the bills. I'll leave the dirty work up to you. Or maybe the clean work."

He turned to go, but as he did he left me with one last word. "From what I've heard, things are only getting started." Then he walked away.

I was going to ask him what that meant, but right then Scott ran up beside me and asked what was going on. I said, "That was James Kuff."

"The butler?"

"Yup."

"What did he want?"

"He said Smith MacNeil is alive."

"He survived the shooting?!"

"Apparently it was all fake."

"Then we need to find him."

"Yes, we do. I want to know why Vesuvius wants him dead."

9:36 AM

Scott and I found Garth, Doug, and Cheryl still in the staff kitchen.

Scott declared, "OK, here's the deal. Smith MacNeil, the YouTuber, is still alive, at least according to some dead guy's butler."

Garth said, "If this were a movie, I would blame said butler for the murder."

"There was no murder," replied Scott. "It was all fake.

Smith faked his death. Live. On YouTube."

"I was referring to the man's former employer, Mr. Stark."

Scott looked at Garth confusedly, so Garth continued. "Never mind, Scott. Go on."

Scott went on. "So, the real thing we need to do now is..." He glanced at me. "What do we need to do, Jeff?"

I said, "Well, since Vesuvius wants Smith dead so badly, there must be a reason, a good reason. Perhaps he has information that can put Vesuvius away. If so, we need to get to Smith first, to convince him to go to the police, because I also want to see Vesuvius behind bars. I would feel better personally if that were to happen."

"Of course, Jeff," said Cheryl.

"Then we'll go get him!" cheered Scott.

"He's probably not home, is he?" said Doug. "I probably wouldn't be."

"You are forgetting," said Garth, "that when Smith MacNeil found out he was being hunted, he went straight home. Perhaps he is there now again, where he feels safe."

"Or if he's not, he might show up at any time," I said.

"Or leave at any time," said Doug.

"It would be great to have surveillance on his house," I said.

The conversation paused while we considered that thought.

"Hey, Jeff, didn't you just get our security cameras working here?" asked Scott.

"Yes," I said.

"What was it called again?"

"Security Tight"

"Ugh. Terrible name. But if we put together some hardware that could monitor Smith's house, you could network it all together, right? So we all could monitor everything live?"

"Uh... I guess I could..."

"Great! So... let's do that?"

I said, "Well, it might need to be battery-powered, since we might not have power there. And it has to connect to the Internet somehow. And it can't be too big. How about we take an hour to try to find some good hardware that can do all those things, then meet again to discuss what we found in an hour?"

"Good plan," said Scott.

"I already have some ideas," said Garth.

Doug and Cheryl nodded.

"OK," I said. "One hour."

10:36 AM

The one-hour timer on my phone started chirp-blonging, so I swiveled my desk chair around. Cheryl walked in at the same time, so I asked "It's an hour. What did we all find?"

Doug said, "I'll start. I found a set of three used security cameras for sale here in town. They plug in with a Cat-6 cable and get power with PoE. I also found a used network switch with a PoE injector. And then for power, I found a small gas generator. And then for Internet, we can also plug in a laptop into the network, and hope there is a strong Wi-Fi signal coming from somewhere."

Cheryl whispered to me, "What's PoE?"

I said, "Power over Ethernet. It's when power goes over the network cables."

"And Cat-6?"

"It's a category of network cable."

"Got it."

Garth replied, "The only problem with that setup, Doug Grimm, is that everyone on the block would not only see it from a mile away, but also hear it."

"Did you find something, Garth?" I asked.

"I did. The latest Raspberry Pi board is my microprocessor

of choice. It can come with a camera module, which lets us record video. Also available is a rechargeable 4000mAh battery, which should be able to power the camera for over fifteen hours, since the camera draws a mere 250mA. For networking, it is possible to purchase a SIM hat which lets you plug in a SIM card, giving you Internet access, just like a smartphone can."

"What's a Hat?" I asked.

"Hardware Attached on Top," Garth replied.

"OK. Well, that sounds good."

"The only unfortunate part of this plan is that all the pieces can arrive at the earliest tomorrow afternoon, and then it will probably take a number of hours to configure everything to get it working."

"And to charge the battery," said Scott.

"Plus I'll add a battery charger to the list," said Garth.

"I don't think we can wait until tomorrow," I said. I scrunched my eyebrows, trying to think of what in the world we were going to do.

"Don't worry about it, Jeff," said Scott. "I've got you covered." We all looked his way, wondering what bizarre idea he was going to suggest. I was sitting next to him for the past hour, so I knew that he wasn't doing any research at all. I had long ago given up on Scott giving us any brilliant ideas. He pulled out his phone and rested it on his knee.

"What's your idea?" I asked.

He pointed at the phone. "That!"

"What?"

"A phone! We use a smartphone! It has a battery, a camera, and Internet access. It's small and quiet." Then he reached for a roll of tape and set it on top of the phone. "There. Now we can tape it to a tree, and bang oh! Done! We've got Smith's front door covered."

"I think it will work," said Doug.

"Of course it will work!" said Scott. "We make things too complicated sometimes."

"OK, let's use a smartphone," I said. "Do we have one available?"

Doug reached for the stack of phones we had sitting around that we used for testing, since we had to make sure our software worked with everything out there. He held one out. "This Adams i26 is good, and has a full battery. And it's running the latest Omniscient."

I took it, then paused. "I guess I'll go set it up then." The guys stared at me. "OK, see you later."

"Call us if anything bad happens to you," said Scott.

I winced, trying not to think about that. "Thanks."

11:13 AM

I had circled the block once already, just spying out where to plant the phone. Now I sat parked a few houses down from Smith's, putting the finishing touches on my plan.

I had considered taping the phone to the trunk of the neighbor's tree, with the tape going all the way around the tree, but that would have been too obvious.

Then I considered propping the phone on a branch, but then I realized that I couldn't reach that branch, and I hadn't brought a chair or anything to stand on.

The next thought was to half bury it in the grass and dirt, but I thought that too would be too noticeable.

Eventually I decided on pulling up my car near the tree, climbing onto the car, then onto a branch on this side of the tree, then over to the other side of the tree and tape the phone there. That might work. Or not.

I drove closer and parked under the tree branch on the road side. Before getting out, I put the phone and tape into my pockets. Then I got out and looked around, hoping nobody would be around. I was wrong of course. There was a teenage girl some distance down the street, coming this way, but her head was angled down towards her phone, probably deeply involved in some quasi-relationship she probably shouldn't be bothering with. But don't ask me about that. I'm a computer nerd—what do I know about relationships? The thought came to me that I definitely should have some solid relationships in my life, and when I thought about that thought, I thought my thought was probably right. But I don't have time for friendships now. I was busy spying on somebody using technology.

I scampered up onto my car, then reached up for the branch and wondered if I would be able to climb up. I found that I could reach my hands around the branch, if I stretched up and leaned off to the side. So I did. Then, with some effort, I was able to reach my feet up and hook them over the branch as well. I crawled hand over hand like this the few feet toward the trunk of the tree, then pulling and pushing on the trunk, and levering various parts of my body around, using muscles I didn't know I had, I was able to claw my way to the top of the branch. I sat there for a while, resting, and letting my scratched-up hands rest.

Good. The plan was working.

Then I stood up on the branch, holding onto the trunk. I could look down onto the top of my car, which looked a long way away even though it was right there. I hugged the trunk, and moved my feet around, one at a time, so that I was standing on the branch on the other side of the trunk. Good. Still working.

I saw the girl again. She was past me, still occupied. I noticed she was typing with her thumbs. I thought that was odd, because I usually just swipe the keyboard with my index finger. Whatever.

I got the tape out and tore off a piece, but that's when I

remembered I had to set up the software now. On the drive over, I was trying to decide if I should just open a video chat with Omniscient, or if I should connect into Security Tight as a security camera. I decided on Omniscient. As I stood there, balancing on a tree, high in the air, holding a roll of tape, and a piece of tape, and a phone, and leaning against the tree, I tried entering my password. When I was halfway through logging in, my personal phone still in my pocket clang-binged as it received a text message. Then a voice from below called out, "Who are you spying on?!"

I jumped so high, I let go of the roll of tape, and almost the phone, but then I half caught it again, but the sticky tape snagged it and pulled it sideways out of my hand. I grabbed for it with my other hand, but missed, and instead knocked it out of my reach completely. It fell to the ground, and not just the grass. It landed on the sidewalk with a very loud crack. I groaned out loud.

Then looking at the man who spoke to me, I said, "Oh. Hi, Smith."

CHAPTER 14

11:45 AM

I didn't know if I should check the text message, talk with Smith, or check the broken phone on the sidewalk, so I said, "Uh... I'll be right down." and started climbing back down the way I came. I added to Smith, "Don't go anywhere. I want to talk to you."

"And I want to talk with you, too. That's why I'm here." He sounded just as Scottish in person as he did in his videos. I was on the other side of the tree. He continued, "Firstly, why are trying to record me? Wasn't it obvious I was dead? I added gunshots and everything."

I held onto the branch, swiveled underneath it, then let go and fell to the ground. It wasn't very elegant, and I felt like I had stretched something in my arms. I was definitely not going to engage in anything more physical for the next while. I said, "James Kuff told me."

"Who's that?"

"He's Yash Nagi's butler."

"Who's that?"

"You don't know who Yash Nagi is?"

"No. Should I?"

"Do you know who Vesuvius is?"

"Isn't that a mountain in Italy?"

"Well, maybe, but it's also someone in charge of a lot of

crime here in the city. And probably elsewhere."

"Never heard of him."

"He's the guy who wants to kill you. Apparently he sent some guys to take you out."

"Did he? I didn't go through all this trouble for nothing then?"

"No, I think you... I... I think I saved your life."

"If that's the case, Jeff, I owe you. I'm hungry. I'll buy you dinner."

Now that I thought about it, I could use some food. And sitting down with this guy would give me a good chance to pick his brain. So I said, "OK."

"Let's take your car. I don't want to touch my stuff at all."

As we got in and started driving, he said, "Have you ever been to Fionn MacCool's?" I shook my head, so he continued. "It's a bit Irish for my liking, but they've got a fine Guinness Steak and Mushroom Stew."

As I started the car, my phone rang, which reminded me that I had received a text message that I hadn't looked at it yet. My phone told me it was Scott, so I answered it. "Hello."

"Jeff. Get yourself back here. We've got major problems. I mean major major."

"What's wrong?"

"Everything's wrong. Nothing is right. I think we've been hacked. For real this time. Like nothing works. Omniscient doesn't connect to anything. Garth is deep into the weeds in the server room. He said his computer isn't on the right VLAN, and you could help with that."

"Are there network problems?" I asked.

"As I said, there are everything problems. Get back here." He hung up.

I said to my passenger, "It seems we have network issues, or something, back at the office, and they want me there."

"Then let's go. If that's where the action is, that's where we should be."

"Um... did you want to come with me to the office?"

"Och, aye! This adventure is only beginning."

12:20 PM

We stopped for Little Caesar's pizza, because you didn't have to wait for them to make it. You just grab it and go. So I downed pepperoni and cheese while I drove. It occurred to me that it might be distracted driving, but I didn't think so.

Smith told me that he used to live in the small town of Gretna Green in Scotland, but when he met with some success being a YouTuber, he moved here. Why here? Because he always wanted to enjoy four distinct seasons a year instead of just two, summer and winter. He said the fall is so beautiful with the tree's red and yellow leaves, and the spring takes its time slowly emerging from the cold of winter.

I had never been far from home in my life, so I didn't know what else was out there, but it felt good that someone liked my country, I guess.

When I said that I wasn't a big fan of the snow and the cold in winter, he said, "If you don't like it outside, go inside."

That sounded like good advice to me.

I parked in the parking lot at The Forks, and as we walked to our office in the Johnston Terminal, I tried sending or receiving chat messages with Omniscient. Nothing worked. In fact, it logged me out. Yes, something was very wrong.

Once on our floor, I found Scott, and was about to ask him what was going on, but he spoke first.

"Smith MacNeil!" he shouted and ran over to shake my visitor's hand, which he did vigorously. "I watch all your videos. It's very interesting! I can't believe you're here! Here! Right here!" He paused shaking his hand to turn around and take a selfie. Then he frowned. "But I can't post this, because everything is down."

"Ay, I heard you had network problems," Smith said.

Scott smiled again, just listening to his accent.

Garth must have heard Smith too, because we heard his voice yelling from the server room, "The network is fine. The servers are having issues."

The three of us joined Garth in the server room. Smith asked, "What issues?"

Garth looked up from behind a server rack, saw Smith, and paused, probably wondering about the security of a stranger being in the server room. But then he continued, "As of right now, I can't even log in to any of them."

"I hope you're not going to format the hard drives and reinstall everything," Smith said.

"On a normal day, that is something I'd consider. But today is not a normal day. All these machines had issues on the exact same day. That can't be hard drive failures."

Smith said, "If you pulled a hard drive, and tried to mount it on a working computer, I wonder what you would see."

Garth held up a hard drive. "I was about to do just that." Then he added, "but thank you for the suggestion."

This raised my eyebrows. Garth was being nice? Maybe something did happen to him.

Garth started plugging cables and adapters into various places, and then he sat down at the desk in front of the screen, typed some stuff, then announced, "The basic folder structure seems fine."

"Do you see any dot TK15 files?" Smith asked.

Garth quickly clacked his keyboard some more and said, "I do. They are everywhere." Then he turned to Smith and spoke slowly, "This isn't what I think it is, is it?"

Smith nodded. "The TK15 files are encrypted versions of all the data the hard drive used to hold. I'm afraid you have been seriously compromised."

12:55 PM

I left the room. I had heard enough. I went to see Nigel, but he wasn't there. I found him in Peter's office. The door was open, but I didn't want to interrupt them. Nigel looked over and saw me, so he asked, "Is the network back up?"

I said, "Apparently the network is fine, but the server's hard drives are full of TK15 files."

"What does that mean?" he asked.

"I think it means we've been hacked, and all our data has been encrypted."

He stared at me. "Seriously? Really?"

I shrugged. "I think so."

He got up and ran out to the server room, and I started to follow him, but heard my name from behind.

"Jeff!" I turned to see Cheryl. She said, "We're getting a lot of calls that people can't use Omniscient. None of their stuff is there, and they can't log in."

"Yeah. It looks like we've been hacked."

"Really?!"

"Yeah. I'm going to go see what's going on."

I was almost back to the server room when Nigel came back toward me. On his way past, he said, "Meeting in the board room, right now. Bring a laptop if you want."

I turned toward my desk, grabbed my laptop, and followed everyone else to the boardroom. On my way past Cheryl's desk, I told her we were meeting in the board room. She said, "I'll leave you boys to it, but what should I tell everyone?"

I shook my head. "Tell them we're working on it."

1:01 PM

We all sat around the boardroom table. I had my laptop, but wasn't doing anything on it. Garth was. He was hunched over, busy with something. So was Ronja. Scott leaned back on his chair. Doug sat silently. Smith was not present.

Both Nigel and Peter were also there. Nigel was talking quickly. "Somebody please tell me the state of the network."

"The network appears to be functioning adequately," said Ronja.

"What about our servers?" asked Nigel.

"Most of our servers cannot be logged into."

"What about the data in our database?"

"The files appear to be encrypted."

"So Omniscient is currently down?"

"Completely."

I plucked up my courage and added, "Cheryl says a lot of people are contacting us about that. We should probably tell them something."

"Perhaps our first act," said Peter, "should be to release a public statement."

"We don't know anything yet," said Nigel.

"We know we're down," said Scott, his hands behind his head. "And so does everybody else."

"But we don't know why," replied Nigel.

"Obviously it's because we got hacked," said Garth.

Nigel frowned. "But we don't know how, or by who."

"'Whom'", Garth corrected.

Nigel's face was slowly getting redder, but Peter interrupted before he could say anything. "This is what we will do. I will make a public statement, and direct our Customer Server personnel on how to respond. I will say we are currently down and are doing our best to recover service. It is not uncommon for online services to be unavailable from time to time. It happens in the industry. I won't mention getting compromised." He stood up. "And when I do that, it will give you some time to get things sorted out. You can take a minute to breathe. As they say in the aviation industry, the first thing you should do in an emergency is to wind your watch. So please relax and wind the watch. Think about and ponder where we are, how we got here, and the best way forward."

As he made his way to the door, I plucked up courage a second time and said, "Peter."

He turned to me, "Yes, Jeff?"

"Uh... when you said 'the best way forward,' it reminded me that we have files encrypted with TK15, and it so happens that we have a TK15 encryption expert here in the office."

He looked around the table. "Who is it?"

"Here's not here right now. He's outside... I mean..." I tried looking through the solid oak door. "Should I get him?"

Peter paused, but then said, "Perhaps you should."

I ran out and found Smith, who was sitting in the staff kitchen, on his phone. I said, "Smith. Please come to the board room. We might need you."

He looked up at me and said, "Och, I'll do it."

We made our way back to the board room, walked inside, and I said to Peter, "This is Smith MacNeil. He is somewhat of an expert on the TK15 encryption algorithm. Smith, this is Peter Steele, our CEO."

Smith said, "Good to meet you, sir!"

"And you, my good man. Jeff says you are an expert, but right now we need someone with a more important quality."

"And what may that be?"

"Someone who can keep a secret. This is a delicate situation. We don't need the world condemning us right now. I'd rather have them think we are working on technical difficulties, than think we are incompetent. Do you understand?"

"Completely, sir."

"Good. Then who is your employer? Perhaps we should contact your company to hire your services."

"I don't have a company, sir."

"You are independent?"

"Ay."

"An IT consultant?"

"I will be honest with you, sir. I have researched the TK15 algorithm thoroughly, but I make my dosh creating videos for YouTube."

Peter was slightly taken aback. Glancing around the room, as if there was evidence lying around, he said quickly, "Perhaps it might be better if you left the room."

"Mr. Steele, even though I make it my living to talk about interesting areas of the technical world, I know what it means to keep me geggie shut. If you want your secrets kept, I'll keep 'em. I give you my word as a Scotsman."

Peter paused, then answered. "Very well, Mr. MacNeil. I accept. I invite you to join our team as a consultant for as long as they think you can be of assistance. You will be fairly compensated. Now if you'll excuse me, I need to go make a public statement."

Peter left the room, then Smith sat down, rested his hands on the table with fingers interlaced, and said, "How can I help?"

1:11 PM

Nigel did his best to sit back and relax in his chair, trying to wind the watch. He took some breaths, but perhaps not quite as deep as they should have been. "There are a number of questions we need answered," he began. "First of all, what is the state of our backups?"

"All of them are compromised," said Ronja.

"All of them?!" replied Nigel.

"Yes."

"What about our remote backups in the cloud?"

"Yes, even those."

"What about our local backups we store in the server

room?"

"Yes, those too."

"How's that possible? I don't think that's possible. I don't think a virus can jump different systems like that."

Garth spoke up and said, "Who said anything about a virus?"

Nigel stopped talking. He blinked. He blinked again. Then he slammed his hand on the table. "We need a list of everyone who has access to all these systems. Ronja, sorry, we start with you, then... Garth?"

Garth said, "The configuration of the VLAN did not grant me access to all systems from my desktop."

"No? I'm pretty sure you have access to everything."

"Not from my desktop. Young Jeff here decided to partition everything into multiple virtual LANs, and I was not on the VLAN that had access to everything. Jeff, however, was on the super network."

"It wasn't my idea," I said. "I was just doing what I was told."

"Classic," Garth scoffed.

Nigel said to everyone, "Raise your hand if you were on the everything network."

I raised my hand. So did Ronja. Garth did not look as angry as I expected him to.

Nigel continued. "Now raise your hand if you knew the password to all the affected systems."

Ronja continued to have her hand up. Garth raised his. I quickly reviewed my memory to see if I had been given all the passwords. Some of them, yes, but not quite all. I put my hand down. Scott and Doug also had their hands down. Of course, so did Smith.

"First of all," began Garth, "regardless of VLAN, if someone in the room here was able to hack into all these systems and steal our data and hold it for ransom, he probably would not admit it by raising his hand."

"Or her hand," added Ronja.

"Secondly," Garth continued, "it is possible, at least in theory, to be hacked from the outside..."

Ronja shook her head. "I don't think it happened from the outside."

"If I may continue, dear system administrator, there is one other possibility that needs addressing."

"If you're thinking of putting my name on the list," said Nigel, "go ahead."

"Not you, sir."

"Then what? Who? I mean whom?"

"Didn't we just hire a security consultant to audit our entire network?"

The room went quiet for a fraction of a second, then we all groaned. Nigel got up and shoved his chair into the table very hard. Then he pulled it back and shoved it in again. He stormed across the room once or twice, and even punched the wall. I looked to see if it left a dent. It did. It occurred to me that he was probably blaming himself, because he was the one who hired Larry.

I also didn't feel good. He was my neighbor. At least I thought he was. That may have all been a lie. Part of me felt vindicated for never really liking the guy, even though God told me to treat him like a friend. "We need to call the police," I said.

Nigel looked at me. "Yes, of course. I'll talk to Peter about that."

"We should also try contacting Larry," said Doug. "He might still reply."

"You're right, Doug," said Nigel. He sat down again and started poking his phone. "Larry," he spoke out loud as he typed, "something happened. We need your help. Please reply or call me." He put the phone down.

Scott spoke up. "Ten bucks says you're not getting a reply to that one."

Nigel's phone vibrated, and he looked at it. "Pay up, Scott. It happened. Larry says this,"I've decided to change careers. I got bored of IT." Nigel scowled and composed a reply, speaking out loud, "It's important. We'll pay top dollar." He put the phone down.

"If you ask me," said Scott, "that was the reply of a guilty man. He's trying to evade."

The phone buzzed again, and Nigel read, "I don't care about the money. I never did."

Nigel suddenly looked very tired. He said, "Maybe this answers a lot of our questions. I'll go talk to Peter about the police. Ronja and Garth, can you please show Smith what's left of our data? Maybe there's something he can do. Thanks, everyone." We all stood up, but then Nigel added, "Oh, Jeff. Why don't you do some real research on this guy Larry. See what you can find on him."

I said, "OK." I would love to.

CHAPTER 15

3:15 PM

Time flies when researching a man who may have kidnapped all your company's data and is holding it for ransom.

I started with everything I knew about him, including everything he ever told us about himself, assuming he wasn't lying.

He seemed to be into speed cubing, so I looked at all the official records for the past many years, but couldn't find any record of him. He may have used a different name, so I also looked for pictures, but couldn't see anybody that looked like him. That did take some time.

The other thing we knew about him, maybe, was that he lost both his parents. They were murdered, supposedly. After more searching, I found a married couple in Toronto that were murdered about fifteen years ago. This incident fit Larry's description of being "bludgeoned to death."

As I was browsing the online article, there was a picture of the couple's fifteen-year-old son. It was a young Larry. I pointed at the screen and said, "I got you!"

"What have you got?" Cheryl asked, as she came into the room.

"I... I found an article about Larry's parents getting murdered, and there's a picture of him." I showed Cheryl the picture.

"That does look like him, when he was much younger. When did this happen?"

"Fifteen years ago."

She nodded. "That would make sense. What else does the article say about it?"

"I haven't read it yet. Tell you what. Why don't you read it while I get a cup of coffee?"

She shrugged, and sat down on the chair I had just vacated. When I got back in two minutes, the rest of the guys were back from the server room, including Smith, who was busy on a laptop.

Cheryl stared at me, looking quite pale.

"What's up?" I asked.

"Do you know what happened?!" she asked.

"No. I was getting coffee." I pointed at the cup. "What happened?"

"He did it!"

"What? Who?" I asked.

"'Whom'," Scott corrected.

"No, Jeff is right," said Garth. "It's 'Who' in this case."

Cheryl continued. "Larry was right that the murder was never solved, but they did have a suspect who didn't get convicted because of lack of hard evidence."

"Who was it?" I asked.

"It was Larry."

"What?"

"Larry killed his own parents."

At this news, everyone else in the room turned to look. Cheryl continued. "Larry was supposedly at a basketball game, but nobody remembered seeing him there. He never showed any signs of authentic grief. They did a psychological assessment, and determined he had antisocial behavior."

"That part doesn't sound that bad." I mean, I might be a

little antisocial myself.

"It's bad, Jeff. It means he's a psychopath."

3:30 PM

Nigel walked into the room. "How are things going, guys?"

I said, "I did research on Larry."

"And?"

"And we found that he is a psychopath who probably killed his own parents."

Nigel stared at us, a little afraid. "Really?"

"Yes."

He walked in a little circle, looking at nothing. "Well... he doesn't work here anymore... And he's not coming back... So... let's try to put that behind us, I guess." he shook his head, trying to change the subject. He looked at the other guys and asked, "How is the data recovery hunt going?"

Garth answered. "We can confirm that there is no ransom note."

"Nothing?" asked Nigel.

"Nothing. We've looked everywhere, including email. It has been four hours. I believe we would have heard something, if there was any intent on behalf of the perpetrator to seek a ransom."

"So someone just encrypted our data?"

"Correct."

"Without asking for a ransom?"

"Affirmative."

"That's crazy. What kind of psychopath does that?"

Nobody answered that question, as the answer was readily available. Then the awkward silence lasted a moment longer as the reality of the situation just dawned on us. Yes, an actual psychopath just encrypted all our data, with no word of ransom, just because he was a psychopath.

Nigel leaned against the door frame to steady himself. Then he shook his head. "It's over. We're sunk. I don't know how we'll recover."

Just as the feeling of loss was overtaking us all, Smith MacNeil spoke up. "Gentlemen. You are forgetting one thing. I have researched extensively the TK15 algorithm. I have also researched extensively the current state of quantum computing. And my research tells me that these two states can be put together."

"You think you can crack the encryption and recover our data?" Nigel asked.

Smith raised his head and stroked his chin, then replied to Nigel, "That's what I'm tell'n you."

"Well... please do! Will you do this for us?"

"I can't promise how long it will take, but I can promise you one thing."

"What's that?"

"It'll cost you. Quantum computing isn't cheap."

"I think it's safe to say the whole company is behind this, so let's say money is not an object at this point."

"Great! Then toss me a credit card; I've got work to do."

Nigel disappeared, presumably to get the payment method.

"What do you need from us, Smith?" Scott asked.

"I'm going to open an account online, then I'm going to upload some quantum code I'm almost done creating. I will also need some sample crypt text, preferably a small file."

"I shall provide that for you, sir," said Garth.

"Thank you, sir," Smith replied. "Now." He turned to the rest of us. "Do you want me to explain exactly what I'm doing, or do you want me to actually do it?"

"I would love to hear what you're doing," said Scott.

Smith raised his voice slightly. "What I'm saying is we don't have time for chit-chat! We need to get down to business."

"Fine. But do you want me to record some video of you doing this?" Scott asked.

Smith relaxed. "Honestly, that would be grand. If this works, I'm willing to come back from the dead, because it will make me a fortune."

4:25 PM

I was doing more research when Cheryl walked in and asked, "How is it going in here, guys?"

"The quantum computers are cooking the soup," said Smith.

"That means they are working to recover our data?"

"Ay, that's what I said, lass."

"Uh... good! Any idea how long it will take?"

"Not the foggiest."

"I mean is it a matter of minutes or hours or days or more?"

He shook his head. "Only the good Lord knows."

She turned to me. "How about you, Jeff? Find anything?"

I nodded. "Yup. Crazy stuff."

She asked, "Like what?" but my phone started ringing. I was going to ignore it, but something inside me nudged me into taking the call. I stood to walk out of the room. "Hello?"

I wasn't expecting the voice that replied, because I thought he was in prison. "Jeff, this is your dad."

"Dad! How did you... I didn't think you were allowed to... what... what's going on?"

"I pulled some strings to get this phone call, and I don't have much time, so listen quickly."

"OK. I'm listening."

"There has been an explosion in the prison."

"What?! Are you OK?"

"I'm fine, but there has been a breakout. I overheard some guards say they want to keep it quiet, so you might not hear about it in the news."

"OK, but why are you telling me? I don't want you to get into trouble."

"It's because of who escaped."

"Who? Or... whom? Or whatever..."

"It was Max. And a bunch of his guys. Jeff, be careful! I gotta go."

The call ended.

I stood there, in the hall, outside our room. I could feel my heart rate accelerate. I could feel my hands starting to tremble. I tried to control my breathing. I had to get myself under control. I wouldn't be any good to anyone if I broke down into a shaking, stammering, hyperventilating pile of anxiety.

I walked up and down the hallway, trying to keep my strength up. In my mind I told God what just happened and tried to listen for a response. The only thing I felt was a tiny bit of peace inside of me. I concentrated on it until it was big enough for my hands to stop trembling.

Then I stopped pacing and took my phone out again. I dialed the number of someone I hadn't talked to in a while. He didn't answer the phone, so I left a message. "Hi, Donald Roberts. This is Jeff Davis. I'm calling you with a news tip. The Stony Mountain Penitentiary just had an explosion. And some inmates escaped. That's about all I know. I think the people need to know about this. Hopefully you can tell them. Thanks." I hung up.

Cheryl just caught me hanging up. "Who was that?" she asked.

"Donald Roberts, the reporter," I said.

"What were you saying to him?"

"I told him what my dad just called and told me. There was an explosion at the prison and some inmates escaped, including Max."

Her eyes went wide. "The guy who tried to kill you?"

I nodded.

"Oh!" She leaned in a gave me a hug, not just for my sake, but for hers too. She may have been holding on a little tightly. That gave me the opportunity to hold her back and comfort her.

"It'll be OK," I said to her. "God takes care of us. He always does."

She nodded.

5:52 PM

The only people left in the office on a Friday evening were us IT people trying to put the world back together.

Ronja was working on getting our local network features working again. Garth just finished installing an instance of Omniscient on a cloud server somewhere, just so we could still communicate with each other. Scott was still around because he didn't have a date this evening, and there was free food. Nigel bought us all supper.

And then there was me. I didn't have a home to go to. And this is where the action was. But perhaps the biggest reason I hung around was because there was at least one person out there trying to kill me. Yeah, I didn't feel a big need to go out right now.

"Is there more cheese quesadilla, Scott?" I asked.

"Nope. All gone," he said. "But there's some chicken left, and plenty of mushroom."

"I like the cheese."

"That's because Habanero Sombrero only uses Bothwell cheese."

"It's good." I selected a piece of chicken quesadilla and dipped it into the chipotle aioli dipping sauce. It was good too.

"What are you going to do about Max on the loose?" Scott asked me.

I shrugged. "Nothing. What is there to do?"

"Go on the offensive and hunt him down."

I laughed and shook my head.

"We could use you as bait," suggested Scott, "and when he comes for you, I'll get him myself."

I looked up at my friend, wondering if he was serious. We locked eyes. Yes, he was serious. The fact that someone out there was willing to take a risk to protect me touched me more deeply than I thought it would. I said, "You would do that for me?"

"Absolutely. In a second."

Doug also spoke up. "So would I." I looked at him, and he was serious too, so I looked back down at the quesadilla and took another bite. Then I said, "Thanks."

Just then Smith came running in exclaiming, "It's finished! It's finished!"

We all looked up in surprise. "It worked?!" Scott asked. "You cracked it? We cracked it? Really?"

"I just got an email saying the program has finished," said the Scotsman. "Now I'm going to go log back in and get the result. If you want, you can all join me."

We scrambled after him, eager to see if this actually worked. I couldn't believe it. We might be back up after only a few hours.

Smith sat at his computer and typed in his username and password, and on the next page, instead of the main dashboard, there was a simple page saying, "Your account has been disabled."

6:19 PM

"What?!" exclaimed Scott. "Disabled?! Why?!"

"Scoundrels!" spat Garth.

"I have no idea," said Smith. "I'll have to call them."

Obviously this man didn't hate the phone as much as I did, because he had no problem punching in the digits and making the call right here right now, without any trace of hesitation. I think I admired that more than the fact that he just cracked the encryption himself with an untested quantum computer algorithm.

After a few seconds he hung up. "Agh. It's late. They're shut." Then he said, "Now what do we do?"

We stood around in silence, wondering what to do next. We couldn't announce that everyone's information was gone, because it had been solved. Presumably, the solution is sitting on a hard drive right now; we just don't currently have access to it. And we can't announce that all the data is recovered, because it is currently encrypted beyond our ability to read it.

Eventually Smith said, "Besides breaking into their facilities and finding the hard drive with our information on it, I can't see what else we can do, except wait for Monday when they're back."

"Omniscient might not survive till then," said Doug.

"Well I'll tell you what I'm going to do," said Scott. "I'm going to go to the washroom."

As he walked away, Garth called out after him, "Unnecessary information, Scott." Then he followed him out, mumbling something about a Dr Pepper. Doug also left, leaving me, Smith, and Cheryl in the room.

I sat down in my chair. "Maybe there is another quantum computing company we can quickly hire."

Smith shook his head. "This is the only company that rents quantum compute online on demand. Everybody else will be shut for the weekend."

"Maybe we could quickly pay them a visit."

"And ask the security guards if we could come in and look

through their computer's database, pretty please?"

That didn't need a response. "Maybe..." but I was running out of ideas. I leaned back and rested my head on the back of chair. I stared at the ceiling.

"I'm going for coffee, then," said Smith and left the room.

I said to Cheryl, the only one still here, "Do you want to leave too?"

"No."

"I don't think I have a solution for you, or for anyone, so I'm not much of a help right now."

"Is that your job? To come up with a solution? To solve this problem?"

"Uh, yes, actually. It is."

"Hmm."

After a minute she said, "God will take care of us."

"OK, good. But until then, should we just put our feet up and do nothing?"

"Not necessarily, no. But if he wants us to do something, he will make it clear."

"Nothing seems very clear right now."

After another minute I pulled out my phone and checked messages. There was one that made me sit straight up. It said, "You didn't think it would be that easy, did you? - Steven McDonald"

6:55 PM

I turned to Cheryl and asked, "Who is Steven McDonald?" but Scott burst in and almost shouted, "Emergency meeting in... in..." He looked around. "In Nigel's office. Right now." Then he disappeared again.

We followed him to Nigel's office. Garth and Doug were already there. Scott closed the blinds and locked the door.

"What's going on?" I asked.

"Something has come up. Something big," said Scott.

"He has spoken," said Garth.

"Who has spoken?" I asked.

Garth pointed up. "The one."

"Oh!" I said. "You heard from God? What did he say?"

Scott answered. "He told us to break into the quantum computer company's office and take our solved answer back."

I looked at Scott to see if he was serious. He couldn't possibly be. But he wasn't smiling. He was looking back at me as if this was real. I said, "Really?"

"Absolutely. We all got the same thing," he said, motioning to Garth and Doug.

I started shaking my head. "I don't think so."

"What do you mean? We did exactly what you said. You said to relax, look for vision, tune into thoughts that come to mind, and write it down. We did that. God told us to break in and get our solution."

I looked at Garth. He said, "It happened. God spoke."

I looked at Doug. He shrugged and said, "I think so, but I don't know."

I said, "OK. I should also mention that it's possible to miss it. It's possible to get something that didn't really come from God. Maybe it came from our own desires, and you think you just heard from him, but you didn't. It was just your mind making stuff up."

Scott shook his head. "I heard it, Jeff. I heard the words. I saw him motioning toward their building. I'm sure of it."

"Maybe you weren't relaxed all the way. There is stress all around us. It's hard to calm down in the midst of excitement."

He continued shaking. "I was relaxed. I heard loud and clear."

"Maybe you let your own desires get in the way. You kinda want to go break in, don't you? We would save the day."

He shrugged. "It's not like I don't want to, but it wasn't on my list until it came to me. He gave me the idea."

"It's dangerous."

"All the more reason to do it."

"It's illegal."

"We obey a higher authority, God himself. He is above the law."

"OK, OK, no, no, that's not how it works. He put our laws in place. We obey him by obeying the local laws."

"That's not how I see it."

"God isn't going to tell us to break the law, Scott."

"He told *me!*"

We stood there, eyes locked for what felt like a long time. Finally I said quietly, "I don't think he did."

Scott backed up a step and threw up his arms. "I have to do what I have to do."

We turned to Garth and I said, "Garth, you can't be serious. You're not really planning to do this, are you?"

He put his hand on his heart. "He met me, Jeff. He spoke to me. I have given him my life. I am his. I am his to command. If he speaks, I obey." He stepped over to side with Scott on that side of the room, leaving Cheryl and me on this side. Cheryl took half a step closer to me, signaling where she stood without words.

Then we turned to Doug, who was still in the middle. I said, "What do you say, Doug?"

Doug looked at Scott and Garth on one side, then at Cheryl and me on the other side. He said, "When my wife... passed away, I did nothing. Now I have the opportunity to do something. I think God told me I need to start taking action. The time for sitting is over, and the time to start using my skills is here."

Scott said, "Then let's go do this thing. Let's take this action."

Doug continued, "However, I respect Jeff, and if he said

God didn't speak, I'm going to trust him." He moved over to our side.

The three of us faced the two of them. I didn't know what to say. Friends should stick together. I would have loved to go with them, but it just wasn't right. I couldn't believe they were serious about doing this. What were they planning to do, break in with guns?

Garth spoke. "Is the fellowship broken?"

"I can't go," I said.

"And I can't stay," said Scott. Without another word, he turned and headed toward the door. Garth followed closely behind.

And just like that, God's network was split in half, with one VLAN for those who stayed, and one VLAN for those who went.

When they were almost gone, I said, "Scott!" He turned. "If you need anything, let us know. Maybe we can help from here."

He seemed to relax a little. "OK," he said, then he nodded. "Thanks, Jeff."

"You're welcome," I replied.

Then they were gone.

CHAPTER 16

7:33 PM

I sat at my computer, waiting for the guys to call or text or something, but there was no word from them at all.

Smith was also there, researching the next big thing, maybe making notes for his return to his online career. "Maybe you should be a YouTuber, Jeff."

I snorted. "That's funny."

"Why do you say that?" He replied. "Because you're an introvert?"

"Yes."

"Well, I'll tell you what. YouTubing is for introverts, and I'll tell you why. When you're filming a video, it's just you and the camera, isn't it? When you're editing, it's just you and the screen, isn't it? When you're uploading a video, you can do that in the toilet, can't you? It's an introvert's dream come true."

"Thanks, but I'll still pass."

"Suit yourself, mate."

"How about you, Doug?" I asked. "You want to be a YouTuber when you grow up?"

"No," he said. I looked over at what he was doing. He was watching some sort of fighting video.

"What is that?" I asked.

"MMA. Mixed Martial Arts."

"I didn't know you were into that."

"Maybe the time for taking action is here."

I doubted he could quickly learn martial arts by watching a video on it, and was about to make a comment to that effect when Cheryl walked in. "Well, we're the last ones here. Everybody else is gone."

"They should be. It's a Friday evening," I said.

Cheryl looked at what I was doing. "Are you still researching Larry?" she asked.

"Yeah. That article we found before never mentioned his name, probably because he was a minor. But I found another article that talks about the same thing, and says his name was not Larry, but Mikey Christopher."

"Maybe Larry is his middle name," said Cheryl.

"I... He gave me his card once." I searched around and found it lying around. "His card says he is Larry Trilbert."

"Maybe he changed his name."

"Huh. That would make sense, if he was trying to escape a past life."

"Yeah," she said.

"Yeah," I replied.

My phone rang. It must be them! Without thinking, I answered it and said, "This is Jeff," but instead of Scott or Garth's voice, it was someone else's.

He said, "Jeff, this is James."

I held my hand over the phone, as if to block the mic, and I whispered to Cheryl, "It's James Kuff, the butler." I stood up and wandered into the hall.

"Hi James. What's up?" I asked, almost tripping over a box on the floor.

"Vesuvius just called us all in. We're all supposed to get together at the new HQ immediately."

"OK."

"Have you heard that there was an escape at the prison?"

"Yes."

"Your friend Max is one of them. There are others, too, including Sven who killed your boss Victor. But I'm not going. I'm taking off. I'm going to disappear. This is the last you'll hear from me. I'm gone."

Here was another reminder of how much my life was in danger. I was almost getting numb to it. Almost, but not quite. "Thanks for the warning, James. I think maybe I'll hang out here at the office for a while. I... I might be afraid to go outside."

"You're at Omniscient now?"

"Yes. Why?"

"Jeff, you're in danger right now. Get out of there!"

"Why? What's wrong?"

"He's going to blow it up. He's going to blow up your building!"

7:46 PM

The call ended.

I looked around at the dimly lit office I had worked in for many years. It was quiet. It was peaceful. It was my last refuge in this world. First I lost my car, then my apartment. Could I really be losing everything I had? It couldn't be real.

I looked around again. It was still peaceful, and outside it was not. Bad things were happening outside. Couldn't I stay inside where it was safe? I sighed.

I found Cheryl and Doug and said, "I was just on the phone with James Kuff. He says this building is going to be bombed."

Cheryl gasped. Doug said, "Like your car and your apartment?"

I shrugged. "I guess so. I don't know. I don't even know if it's true, but James thinks it is."

"I would rather find out if it's true from the outside rather than from the inside."

Cheryl nodded. I said, "Of course you're right." I sighed again. "I'll go tell Smith, then let's evacuate."

"I'll get my laptop," said Doug.

"Me too," said Cheryl.

I found Smith and told him about the bomb threat. He said, "I already escaped death once today. I'll do it again if I have to."

We both collected our things, then found the other two, and made our way to the front door. As we walked out, Smith said, "Usually people run for their lives away from a bomb. That's what they do in the movies, at least. Maybe they should make this into a movie. If they do, I want to be played by Ewan McGregor."

We carried our stuff through the big glass doors, and then paused at the elevator. As we stood there waiting, I mentioned casually, "You know, if the building blows up, we might get stuck in the elevator or something."

"The stairs are free," said Doug.

So we moved away from the elevator and started down the stairs. We even heard the ding as it arrived, but we trudged down anyway. Once we were outside in the evening air, the idea of an emergency was hard to hold onto. It was a fine Friday evening.

When we were a small distance away from our building, the Johnston Terminal, I said, "I guess I should call the police or something and tell them about the bomb threat."

I put down my laptop and pulled out my phone. As I was about to make the call, the third floor of the Johnston Terminal exploded in a deafening roar of volume, high-pressure air, glass, and other material debris. We were knocked to the ground. In the confusion, I must have hit my head or something, because I had a hard time getting back up. As I instinctively looked for my phone, I heard screaming. It was coming from Smith, who was lying on the ground, grabbing his neck where a large piece of glass was protruding from it.

"Don't pull it out!" Cheryl yelled, as she went to his side to help. I was glad she was OK. Doug also seemed fine, considering we were almost just blown up.

"Lie still!" Cheryl said. "Don't pull it out." His neck was red with blood, and he was bleeding onto the ground. She tried to put some pressure on the wound to keep it from bleeding, and it seemed to be working.

As we tried to catch our breaths, Doug said to me, "Jeff, you saved our lives."

I nodded. "James did."

"It looks like Smith needs help," said Doug. "I'm going to call 911."

Judging by the people starting to gather at the scene, I suspected 911 had already been called, but we did too. I looked up at the place we had all worked for many years. I couldn't really see our floor, except through the blown-out windows, but I could imagine it was gone. What did this mean? What would become of us? We almost died. Maybe we will still die. I had to sit down.

As I did, a stranger handed me my phone. The screen was cracked in several places, and a corner was broken off, but miraculously it seemed to still work perfectly fine. I said, "Thanks."

In a few minutes the ambulance arrived. Smith was still conscious and even talking. As they loaded him onto a stretcher, I said to him, "I think you're going to be all right, Smith."

"My first death was a lot easier than this one," he said. "I should have been recording. This will make a great video. I look forward to meeting Ewan McGregor."

As they closed the ambulance doors, it occurred to me that

I should ask him about what to do when the guys find the encryption key. They're still out there. And now we have no home base.

8:47 PM

Cheryl and I were in the front seat of her car. Doug was in the back. We just sat there, not knowing what to do, trying to comprehend what just happened. Our building had just exploded and Smith almost died. I wanted to go up and check on our servers, but the police wouldn't let us. We had given them our statements, but it turns out they didn't care that much about us, because we were just three witnesses among a large crowd. I didn't tell them about the tip-off from James, but of course they didn't ask. If they had asked, "Did anybody warn you that the building was going to explode?" I probably would have said, "Yes," because that's the right thing to do, but nobody asked.

I sat holding my cracked phone in my left hand, just in case the guys would call and tell us how they were doing. My attention was divided between what just happened here and what was happening with Scott and Garth.

My phone twi'danged.

I glanced down and saw that I had gotten a text message. Cheryl looked over, and Doug said, "Anything interesting?"

I said, "It's from Scott. He says, 'We need help.'"

"What does that mean?" asked Doug.

"That's all it says," I replied. "We need help."

"There are many kinds of help," said Doug. "Maybe they need help factoring a large number."

"Maybe they're in trouble," said Cheryl.

"But what are we supposed to do?" I said out loud.

"We'll have to ask God what to do," Cheryl said.

"Yeah", I agreed. I closed my eyes and tried to imagine

God there somewhere with me. I couldn't imagine him in the driver's seat, because Cheryl was there. I tried to imagine him outside, crouched over, looking through the window at me. That didn't work either. Then suddenly I saw him in my mind, lying across the hood of the car, head in hand, munching on an apple. The silent conversation went something like this.

"Hi," I imagined saying to him.

He held up the apple in a gesture of greeting, winked, then kept on eating.

"Wait... you're eating an apple while the world here is literally falling apart?"

"It's not falling apart. I saved you from the explosion, didn't I?"

"I thought that was James."

"Who do you think told him to call you at just the right time?"

"James Kuff can hear from God now, can he?"

"Everybody can hear from me if I talk loud enough. With some people, like James, I shout, with some people, like you, I whisper."

"Why would you whisper to me?"

He moved closer, almost touching the windshield, and he whispered, "Because I want you to lean in to me, to get close to me, to get close to my heart, to feel my breath upon you, to feel my arms wrap around you in love."

I surrounded, and imagined being close to him and wrapping my little arms around him, and feeling his presence. Then I sat back down in my chair and asked, "So what should we do now?"

God went back to eating his apple and casually mentioned, "Do whatever you want. That's what you've been doing up till now."

"What?! Come on! I thought we've been trying to follow you, not doing whatever I want."

"Have you really been trying to follow me? Scott and Garth are."

I was awakened from my conversation with God by Doug stating from the back seat, "I still think God wants us to break into Future Tech."

I closed my eyes again and tried to get back into it, but it was fading fast. The last thing I could imagine was God pointing a finger at me. No, it wasn't at me, it was at the dashboard in front of me. Was that a piece of paper?

I picked up the paper from the dashboard and said, "What's this?"

Cheryl answered, "Oh, that's stuff Dad had on him when they brought him in. They gave it to me. I don't know what it is."

When I opened it up and scanned it, I read a contract that gave permission to Omniscient to perform penetration testing on FutureTech, signed by Daryl Bankowsky and Robert Alexander. I read it again. What?! This... this... this was incredible! But how? Why? Then I remembered and turned to Cheryl and said, "This is the paper your dad was signing when I came to visit the other day."

"Yeah. So?"

"So, it gives us permission to perform pen testing on their building."

"What are you saying?"

"I'm saying it's no longer illegal for us to break in." I waved the paper. "We have their permission."

Doug leaned forward and said, "I know exactly what we need to do."

9:40 PM

When Daryl Bankowsky's daughter, Cheryl, turned sixteen, he didn't give her the usual gift a wealthy father gives his daughter, such as a pony or a luxury car. No, he gave her something he thought might actually help her in life, something that would toughen her up a little, something that would cause her to dig deep inside of herself and come up with the courage to do something that most people never do, which was in this case, risking her life by jumping out of an airplane. He bought her skydiving lessons. And she took them. And she passed.

When Doug Grimm's wife died after they were married for twenty-four years, he decided to confront the cowardice in himself that got her murdered. He did things like learn gun control, and take various evening courses in fencing, and self-defense. To confront his fear of death, he also took a course in skydiving. It turned out he enjoyed that one so much that he got licensed by the CSPA to do tandem jumps.

And that explains how an hour later the three of us were sitting in the back of his friend's little plane, getting ready to jump out. This was Doug's brilliant idea. Because if you need to do pen testing on a building, obviously the best way to do it is to parachute down on top of the building, just before it gets dark.

The only way they barely talked me into doing this was because I felt bad for saying "No" before, when God actually wanted us to go.

So there we sat on the floor of this tiny plane. The pilot had the only seat. Behind him, the three of us huddled together. Cheryl was already suited up, complete with a helmet, jump suit, and a parachute strapped onto her back. I tried not to get distracted by how good she looked in that jumpsuit.

Doug and I were also suited up, except that I wasn't strapped in yet, which meant I got to look out the window. I was surprised by how familiar everything was. The view of the city looked exactly like Google Maps, except that the resolution was a lot higher.

The plane lurched, sending fear and trepidation into my stomach. I considered telling them that we should turn back, but decided against it. I had made that same decision many times already. Instead, I tried to imagine God here with us. The only thing I saw was him sitting there, reading a newspaper and chuckling.

It made me feel a little better, but when he shook his newspaper, as if to draw attention to it, I thought maybe I would read the news too, to distract myself. So I did.

Through my cracked screen, I scrolled past celebrity relationships, natural disasters, Bitcoin, and business news. I stopped when I saw a headline entitled "Steven McDonald named new CEO of FutureTech" The article talked about the new CEO who was appointed by the board. Apparently he was one of the biggest shareholders, and it suggested that he influenced the board to name him successor, seeing as he played a big part in putting those board members on the board. The article went on to describe how Steven made his wealth, which was largely by mining cryptocurrency. It said that he was single and lost both his parents when he was young.

Then I scrolled farther down and saw a picture of him.

I yelled over the roar of the engine, "Uh, guys!" but I was drowned out by the commotion behind me. Doug was strapping me in.

"Guys!" I yelled again, but Doug just opened the door. Wind flooded in, drowning out everything.

I held up my phone and pointed to the picture of Steven McDonald, but I only heard Doug yell in my ear, "You need to put it away. We're jumping now."

I shook my head and reached to close the door, but it was too late. Doug had already moved me into position. My legs were dangling out the door. I kept pointing to my phone.

Cheryl crawled into position to look at what I was pointing at. She yelled, "What about him?"

I yelled, "This is the new CEO of FutureTech."

She looked at the phone again, then back at me, then said, "That's a picture of Larry."

I nodded. "He must have changed his name again, and now he's CEO of FutureTech. And we're breaking into his company. I don't think we should do this."

Cheryl didn't say anything, but turned to look at Doug, directly behind me. Doug said, "I know what to do. God already showed me."

I said, "What?"

"He wants me to push you out of the plane." Then he pushed me out of the plane.

9:59 PM

As soon as my bottom lost contact with the floor of the plane, my body realized that it was suddenly neither sitting nor standing, and automatically tried to stand on something. My legs pumped, looking for purchase, but found nothing. Doug tapped me on the shoulder, which was our reminder for me to spread out my arms and legs just like we briefly practiced. I did so, and felt not quite as out of control as before, because I was actually doing something. I know I wasn't actually helping anything—I was just falling straight down toward the city. Doug was doing all the work of balancing us.

Then he must have pulled the chute, because I felt a big tug and my legs were pointed down again instead of sideways.

I could see FutureTech's building. There were no lights on the top of the building, but there were around the edge. And the parking lot was lit. We were headed for the roof, which was getting dark, but still barely visible.

Doug didn't do any fancy acrobatics, and he didn't let me

steer. He just pointed us there, then as we approached the roof, he yelled for me to lift my legs. I did, pointing them out in front of me, and we landed with me on my bottom again, and him on his knees.

As relieved as I was to be back on terra firma, even if it was the roof of a building, I was even more relieved to look back and see Cheryl coming in for a landing beside us. Yup, she still looked good. It was only at this point I could breathe easy again, after I caught my breath, of course.

I ran over and gave her a big hug and a kiss. "Aren't you glad I didn't die?" I asked.

She laughed as she took off her jumpsuit. "You're not going to die."

"I could have. A lot of things could have gone wrong." I unzipped my jumpsuit as well.

"Jeff, I know you're not going to die. Not yet, anyway."

"How can you be so sure?"

"I just know." She smiled at me.

As I stepped out of the first pant leg of the jumpsuit, something from my own pocket fell to the ground.

"What's that?" Cheryl asked, but before she had a chance to get a good look at it, I nabbed it off the ground as Doug came over.

"What's the purpose of this mission?" he asked.

I quickly pocketed the item, and said, "As of an hour ago, I thought it was to help Scott and Garth, who apparently need our help."

"And get our decryption code," added Cheryl, "to save Omniscient."

I paused to think about Omniscient, which didn't have a building anymore and how we would survive, but I didn't have time to think about that now. So I said, "But now I'm wondering if we should just find Scott and Garth and get out safely."

"Safe sounds good to me," said Cheryl.

"Either way starts by finding the guys," said Doug. "We can decide what to do next after we find them."

"OK," I said.

"But now I have one question," said Doug.

"What?"

"Do we treat the security here as hostile? Or do we still continue with pen testing?"

Cheryl looked at me. I looked at her, then we both looked at Doug, who looked back at me. I said, "Let's continue pen testing for as long as we can."

We all nodded.

We stashed our parachuting stuff in the shadows of a corner, then grabbing our pen testing equipment, we left our huddle and made our way to the door on the roof.

We soon found our first obstacle as pen testers, a locked steel door.

CHAPTER 17

10:10 PM

There was a small room on the roof of the building, which contained, presumably, the stairs going down. It was locked, of course.

As Doug opened his backpack, he said, "Check under the door to see if it is free."

"What do you mean?" I asked.

"Can I slip something underneath the door, or is it blocked by anything?"

I ducked down and felt and looked as well as I could, but saw nothing under the door. "It looks clear to me."

Then Doug bent down with me, and pushed something underneath the door. It was a long piece of metal with a curved hook on the end. He slipped it almost all the way under and started fiddling with the end still in his hand. He said, "I'm trying to grab the handle from the inside."

I understood, so I nodded. I think Doug must have done this before.

It took a minute, but we soon heard a click, and the door came open. He shook his head. "I haven't done this in a while. I'm rusty."

"You did great, Doug," said Cheryl.

We went in, then down the stairs, then through another door that wasn't locked.

A hallway stretched to the left and to the right.

"What should we do first?" I asked. "Find the server room? Find the guys?"

"Maybe we should find a network jack, and see what's in their network. Maybe we can find our decryption key there somewhere."

I nodded.

We went down the hall, checking doors. Most of them were locked, but Cheryl found one open, so we went inside. It was an office with a typical desk facing the door. The lights in the room were off and we kept it that way. Sitting on the floor, on the far side of the desk, Doug and I pulled out our laptops. Cheryl kept watch by the window.

There was a desktop computer in the room plugged into the network. Thankfully there was also a network printer in the room, which meant Doug and I both got our own plugs.

Wired networks typically don't have passwords like Wi-Fi networks do, so that gave us an advantage. We spoke out loud as we discovered things.

"It's a 192 dot 168 dot 3 network," said Doug.

"I'll bet they have a subnet for every floor, and we're on the third floor," I said.

He nodded.

After a few minutes of poking around I said, "Oh, look. They're running Security Tight."

"I don't suppose you could get access to it. It would be great to see all their security cameras and locks and everything."

I shook my head. "I can only get as far as the password screen, and I don't know the password. But maybe they have open access to everyone coming in on a different network, like we do with ours."

Doug nodded. "That would be handy. That way we would only need one password to get access to everything. I'll get started cracking the Wi-Fi passwords."

"How are you going to do that?" Cheryl asked.

"Well, with the Wi-Fi card in this laptop I can listen for traffic, and I can also mess with it. It's not possible to simply listen to someone log in and get the password. That's too easy. But what I can do is kick someone off the network and hope they automatically log back in." Doug examined his screen, then smashed a button on his keyboard. "Kicked…" A few seconds later he smiled. "…and logged back in, probably automatically. And that little transaction was recorded."

"Now you got the password?" Cheryl asked.

"No, but now I have something I can brute force. It will take a few minutes to crack it."

"Are you going to crack it on that laptop?" I asked.

"Yes. It has a nice GPU. How's it going with your looking around? Have you found anything besides Security Tight?"

"No. This network is probably on a VLAN that is locked out of all the good stuff."

"The nerve of these people, locking down their network. Don't they know we're trying to break in? Who's idea was this, anyway, to use VLANs?"

I know Doug was just joking, but I replied anyway. "Um… maybe Larry, the network security expert and the new CEO."

"Oh, yeah. Right. But he hasn't been CEO for very long, so maybe there is still a chink in the armor somewhere."

"Like what?"

"Like a separate Wi-Fi network that gives access to everything if we have the password. Let's go find the server room."

10:35 PM

We packed up and left the office, heading down the hall. "Let's find an elevator," said Doug.

As we walked, I noticed there were security cameras at the ends of the hallways. "I'm surprised nobody has come to check on us, considering all these cameras," I said.

Doug nodded. "Maybe that means the security guards are all busy."

"Is that good or bad?" I asked.

"Maybe they're busy with Scott and Garth," suggested Cheryl.

That thought didn't make me happy.

We arrived at an elevator and Doug said, "Oh, good. Monarch."

"What?" I asked.

"Monarch makes these elevators." Doug reached into his pocket and pulled out two stickers. They had red stripes and the words "Monarch Elevator" on them. He stuck one to his shirt and gave one to me. I stuck it on, too. "If anyone asked, we are Monarch elevator repairmen."

"Am I a repairman too?" asked Cheryl. Did I detect a hint of attitude in that question?

"I only had two stickers," said Doug. "You can be our assistant in training."

I added my comments. "Garth would say she's a repairman. Kaleisha would say she's a repair person."

Doug rolled his eyes, "Oh, let's not get into that."

I chuckled.

Doug punched the elevator button and we waited.

Suddenly feeling a bit sour inside, I said, "I don't really like the idea of lying. If God is the truth, we should be on the side of truth, not falsehood."

"We have a legal agreement," said Doug. "We are allowed to do pen testing. We have their permission."

I shrugged. "Maybe, but it doesn't make me feel any better."

The door opened and we stepped inside. Doug punched

the basement button.

As the doors were closing, a man wearing a suit and carrying a cardboard box came from around the corner and jumped into the elevator. Then the doors closed. He smashed the main floor button.

The three of us looked at each other, wondering what we were supposed to do, which was maybe nothing.

But Doug started talking to the man. I suppose the best defense against getting caught is a good offense. "Working late" Doug offered, as the elevator moved down.

"More like not working," the suit replied. "A pile of us just got laid off."

"The new CEO is really shaking things up, huh?" Doug replied.

"You got that right. And just as our quantum service was taking off." He sniffed and shrugged. "I don't care. I don't work here anymore."

The elevator stopped and the door opened. I started to feel relieved when the man walked out, but it was short-lived, because Cheryl darted out after him. Not wanting to get separated, and getting caught off guard, I followed along. I heard her say to the suit, "I'll hand in your security badge for you. I'm going to the front desk anyway."

The man looked at her happy, smiling face, shrugged, then unclipped his badge from his shirt and handed it to the pen tester. I heard him say, "Whatever," then turn and walk off in a different direction.

As Cheryl walked back toward us, trying not to swagger, she waved a badge at us and grinned. I guess she had good reason to gloat, but I barely noticed, because I was completely occupied with the site behind her.

Behind my beautiful girlfriend, I could see what looked like the front doors of the building, and coming through them was a posse of tough men. They looked like they came fresh off the bus from jail. I immediately turned around and walked straight toward the elevator. Soon Cheryl was there too, still grinning.

I said, "I just saw a bunch of men come through the main doors. They looked dangerous." The elevator moved down.

"I saw them, too," said Doug.

"Let's find the guys and get out of here," I said.

"First I'll trade this badge for your elevator sticker," said Cheryl.

I gave her the sticker and clipped on the badge.

The elevator door opened and as I started walking out, I came face to face with a large security guard dressed in black. He didn't seem happy to see me. He glared down at each of us and said, "What's going on here?"

10:42 PM

I stammered and spat out, "I, uh.. we're here to work on the elevators." I caught him looking at my badge, so I said, "I mean, they are here to work on the elevators. I'm showing them around."

"You're from sales," he said. "Why isn't someone from properties doing that?"

I shrugged. "I was here. They asked me."

"We need to find the server room," said Doug. "We've lost contact with the South lift. There might be a problem with a router or network appliance. If you could show us where that is, we would appreciate it."

The man glowered at Doug. "Why wasn't I told about this?"

"I don't know," Doug replied coolly. "You should have been. We only got the call ourselves less than an hour ago. Must be a breakdown in communication. We apologize for that. But we're here now. Can we see the server room please?"

The man almost growled, but seeing the Monarch stickers, he had to comply. I suppose he knew very well himself about the new CEO's shake-up, so Doug's explanation probably sounded plausible.

"This way," he said, and started down a hall. The three of us followed.

I admit I was nervous, but Doug seemed to be able to keep his cool, probably because he had done pen testing before, and besides, we technically were allowed to do this.

Suddenly Cheryl called out to Doug who was walking in front, "Maybe I should go back to the South lift and you should stay there, then we'll try to connect that way."

Doug and the security man stopped and turned around. Doug looked like he was trying not to be confused and said, "OK. Let's do that." Cheryl turned around, and grabbing my arm as she went, pulled me back, as Doug and the man continued on.

"What's going on?" I asked.

"Did you happen to glance into this room we passed?" she asked.

"No."

"Well, look." We stopped and she gestured in. The door we stopped at had a glass window in it, and I could see in. The label "Security" was also on the door. I looked in, past the main room, into another room on the far side. The door was half open, and I could see two men sitting on the far side of a desk. It was Scott and Garth.

"He's coming!" Cheryl whispered loudly.

I glanced, and saw the security man coming back. Cheryl was already walking toward the elevator. I followed her, trying to control my breathing, and trying to think at the same time. Doug was on his own right now, hopefully in a server room, so he's fine. Cheryl was about to pretend to work on an elevator. She could use some help, but I'm not sure what I could offer her. Garth and Scott might actually be in trouble. Maybe there was something I could do about them, but first I had to lose the security guard behind me.

We were coming to the end of the hall, and I could turn left or right. I had a fifty-fifty chance of losing him. I could hear him coming up behind me fast. I had to make a decision. Maybe I should stop and tie my shoe. Nope. That would be too obvious. Then I had a brilliant idea.

I ran up to Cheryl, who was standing in front of the elevator buttons and looking a little nervous. I leaned my elbow up against the wall and pretended to be interested in her. "So," I said, trying to sound attractive and masculine, "have you been at Monarch a long time?"

She grinned, cluing in to what I was doing. "A few years, I guess."

"What's it like working in a male-dominated industry, being such an attractive woman such as yourself?"

She smiled back at me, and was about to say something when the security guard came up to us and said to Cheryl, "Excuse me ma'am. Is this gentleman bothering you?"

She shook her head. "Oh, no. No. Not at all. He can stay as long as he likes."

He turned to me and almost frowned again. "Let me know if you need anything."

"Thanks. I will," she said.

I watched him go, then Cheryl said to me, "That was quick thinking."

"Thanks. It wasn't really hard, you know, pretending to be attracted to you." I took a step toward her and gave her a quick kiss on her forehead.

"We don't have time for this," she said. "Go check on Scott and Garth."

I nodded. "Right," I said, then set off to try to save my friends from some unknown danger.

_10:59 PM_

Soon I was back at the door with the window, and looking in. I could still see the guys. They were just sitting there looking up at the ceiling. I wondered if they were tied up. I wondered if they were being guarded. I wondered if I could do something to the guard. I probably couldn't take him out physically, but maybe I could distract him, or lure him away. But then the guys would still be tied up, maybe. Maybe I could distract the guard and leave them a knife or something. I had a pocket knife in my backpack. I quickly took it out and held it in my hand. Then I put it in my pants pocket because I didn't want to look threatening.

I opened the door and walked in, trying to stay as quiet as possible for as long as possible. There was nobody in this room, but that other room might have a guard in it. I tried sneaking up to it by staying visible to the guys but not anyone else. When I got near, Scott saw me, bugged out his eyes in surprise, then glanced back to the someone across the desk. Scott then looked back and me and gestured frantically for me to get away, but it was too late. A guard, also dressed in an all-black uniform, suddenly opened the door all the way, and stared at me.

"Can I help you?" he demanded.

"Yes, hi. You can."

"Who are you?" he asked.

"Me? Oh, I'm…" I was about to say Jeff, but then realized that I probably wasn't. Thinking fast, I said, "I'm from sales," then I held up my badge and glanced at it myself. "I'm Matt."

"What do you want?"

"Well, you see, I came back for my laptop, so I could get some work done on the weekend, but then I remembered that I had accidentally left it in someone else's office, a colleague of mine, but when I went there, the door was locked, of course, so I thought maybe you could unlock the door for me, since you are security." Then I stared at him and he drilled his eyes into mine, trying to discern my inner most thoughts and intentions.

Finally he said, "Which office?"

"It's just down the hall here." I gestured with my hand.

"Can you identify it?"

"It's one of those gray ones."

He growled to himself, then said, "Alright. Let's make it fast."

I backed up slightly to let him go first, and just as he turned his back to me, I took the knife from my pocket and threw it at the guys. I had terrible aim and it hit the wall above them, clattering loudly.

The guard heard it and went back to look at them, but not seeing anything wrong, he turned to go again.

I let out a breath of relief and said, "Who are those guys?"

"None of your concern. Let's get your laptop."

I said, "OK", and followed him out, glancing back once more at the guys who were smiling. I think I succeeded.

As we walked down the hall, he again asked, "Which room?"

I was going to pick one at random, but then it occurred to me that the guys would want to escape, so I should pick one around the corner. "I think it's just here around the corner," I said.

Once around the corner, I picked one at random and pointed to it. He took out a ring of keys from his pocket. I was hoping there would either be a stray laptop lying around, or there wouldn't be and I would pretend to be surprised and confused.

He opened the door and stood there, waiting for me. I went in and looked at the desk. "It was right here!" I looked under the desk, behind the chairs, and everywhere else I could think of, even in some cupboards. There was nothing, of course. "What? Did I actually take it with me? I don't understand."

"It's clearly not here, so let's lock the door again."

On my way out, I said, "Well, thanks anyway. I appreciate it."

He locked the door, then said, "Hey."

I turned to look at him.

He pointed at me. "It's late. Go home."

"Yeah. OK."

I started to go back the way we came, but then thought better of it and turned the other direction, just to get as far away from him as possible when he finds Garth and Scott missing.

As soon as the guard was gone I ducked into a room off the hall. It looked like a staff kitchen, completely deserted, of course. I stopped and caught my breath. I needed to come up with a plan, but not quite yet, because I first needed a washroom. Spying one on the far side of the room, I made my way there, but when I was about to open the door, it opened itself and before I could do anything, I was standing face to face with my half-sister Veronica.

CHAPTER 18

11:16 PM

"Jeff! What are you doing here?" she exclaimed.

"I... I... Veronica," I answered.

She stomped past me, toward the door, probably to tell someone I was there.

I said, "Wait!"

She rolled her eyes. "What for?"

"We need to talk."

"Yeah right."

"It's important... I...", I began, but she wasn't listening. I had to say something powerful, and quickly. "I know who your father is."

She turned and drilled me with her eyes, then said, "B.S."

"It's true. He said he's been following you all your life."

As she stared at me in silence, I didn't know if she was going to bolt or not. I sat down at a table and said, "Come, sit. Let me tell you about it."

She slowly pulled a chair out and sat on it, arms crossed. I took that as my cue to start talking.

"I was talking with my dad the other day," I began. Veronica's expression didn't change. "You know he left us when I was fifteen."

"Get on with it."

"Anyway... but even before that he said he had an affair

with another woman."

"Let's move this along a bit faster. I have things to do."

"OK... and I... I mean..."

She stood up.

I didn't have time to beat around the bush. "It was your mom," I said. "My dad is your dad."

Her hardened exterior cracked, then softened, then got angry. She said, "Bull!", but it wasn't convincing. You could tell that she was going over the idea in her mind. She worked for him for a long time. Maybe she was rethinking all the times he treated her well for no reason. "He never told me!"

I shrugged.

"If this is true," she said all sorts of emotions criss-crossing over her face, "It means..."

"It means I'm your brother. Well, half brother. Haven't you always wanted a brother?"

She ignored the question, still trying to make sense of this new world. "It means I have family." She rubbed her abdomen. I glanced down to where she was rubbing. I had thought she was just gaining a few pounds, but now I noticed she didn't look fat anywhere else.

I said, "Veronica?"

She asked, "What?" as if she were actually curious.

I said, "Are you pregnant?"

She pointed her finger at me and tried to sound tough. "That's none of your business."

I said, "Yes it is my business if..." I paused to get used to the idea myself, then continued. "...if I'm going to be an uncle. I want to be a good uncle. And brother."

The suddenness of being surrounded by family who might actually care for her, coupled with the fact that her secret now no longer had to be carried around only on her shoulders was too much for her. Her face scrunched up momentarily, then she said, "I don't want to be a bad mom."

I didn't know what to do with a crying woman in front of me, so I got up and offered her a hug. She accepted and wrapped her arms around me. As I returned the embrace and felt her long black hair on her back, I remembered Cheryl's dream of the dark-haired woman being attracted to me. I guess that was Veronica. But the other part of her dream was of a bunch of people following me. I guess those were the other guys here in the building with me. Maybe I was supposed to be leading this team, which I wasn't at the moment.

I let go and said, "I have to go."

She nodded. "Me, too."

Then I remembered what my dad had said. I said, "Veronica. You need to stop working for Vesuvius, or whoever it is you're working for. He's bad news. He's only using you to get to me, or Dad, or both of us. When he's done with you, he'll get rid of you. You need to take care of yourself by getting away as fast as you can. You need to take care of both of you."

She smirked. "First of all, Jeff, I know he's bad news, OK? And second..." She took a deep breath and let it out. "Yeah, I'm going to take care of us, both of us. I will now." She turned to go, but first said, "When this is all over, let's talk."

I nodded. "Yeah. Let's."

She nodded too. "Good," she said, then started toward the door. Halfway there, she added, "Don't die!"

"Thanks," I replied. "I'll try not to."

Veronica might be taken care of, but there were still four of my friends somewhere in this building, and I had a feeling they needed me. I set off to find them, and hoped not to die in the process.

11:33 PM

I found my way back to where Cheryl and I had left Doug to go to the server room. I kept walking, and found the server room myself. The door was open, so I went in.

There were several racks of computers, each plugged into dozens of network and power cables. The cables ran underneath a false floor. I suppose that was easier than putting them up on the ceiling. Around the room, there were also some desks and computer stations. Also, I noticed, the room contained Doug, Cheryl, Garth, and Scott. Garth looked up and said, "Ah, the fellowship reunites."

Scott came over and gave me a hug. "Thanks for rescuing us, Jeff. That was brilliant!"

I smiled and shrugged. Then I remembered to try to be a leader or something, so I closed the door, then asked, "So, how's it going?"

"Still working on the Wi-Fi passwords," said Doug. "How about you, Garth?"

Garth said, "I believe I have found where on the network the customer accounts are stored, but I can't read them from that location. I am currently wandering around the ether looking for a way in."

"I don't mean to rush you," I said, "but we really need to find what we're here for and get out."

"I'll attempt to wander faster," said Garth.

"Doug, did you say 'passwords' plural?" I asked.

"Yes," he replied, "There are several Wi-Fi networks: 'future_guest', 'future_staff', and 'future_super'."

"You don't think the future_super network might be the God Network we're looking for, do you? The one that provides access to everything?"

At this suggestion, Scott and Garth also looked up. Scott said, "God network?"

Garth replied with, "Certain pieces of software, peripherals, or even servers, can be configured to not require a password when the user is coming in on a certain network. This way you only need access to the network, and you can do anything."

"Wow," replied Scott. "That sounds...powerful."

"Too powerful in my opinion," said Garth.

I thought for a moment, then said, "Maybe we should focus our energy on getting into that Wi-Fi network. That might be our best bet to get the password to get our encrypted data back. Then we need to get out of here."

"We have a small problem there," said Doug. "Nobody is currently connected to future_super, so I can't kick someone off to reconnect to examine the network traffic."

I frowned, then started pacing back and forth. "Well, we need to think of something." Then I added, "That would also give us access to security cameras and doors and such, not that we really need that, but it might help us escape."

The guys kept on doing their thing, while I talked out loud. "It would make sense that Future Tech is using software called Security Tight."

"Why?" asked Cheryl.

"Because they are both dumb names. Now 'Omniscient'– that's a good name. Everything's got to have a good name."

Scott piped up, "Then what's God's name?"

"What?" I asked.

"If everything has to have a good name, what's God's name? 'God' is actually pretty generic."

"The Lord?" suggested Cheryl.

Garth replied with, "'Lord' is simply a term referring to anyone with authority or power, such as a landlord. Placing a 'the' in front of it might tell us to whom you are referring, but doesn't do much for a specific name."

"Jesus?" suggested Scott.

Garth replied again. "The name Jesus is simply the Greek form of the Hebrew name Yeshua, or Joshua. It was a common name. But to rephrase the question, Jesus of Nazareth was the son of whom exactly?"

"OK, Garth," said Cheryl, "why don't you just tell us God's name yourself?"

"Simple," he began, but he never finished, because we were all interrupted by security guards bursting into the server room, guns in hand.

11:51 PM

"Step away! Step away from the computers!" they shouted at us. They weren't actually pointing their guns at us, probably for legal reasons, but they had them out and prominent. It made me nervous. "Out! Everybody out of the room!" It probably made me compliant, too. Maybe I should have run away. But it was too late now.

The guard nearest me placed his hands on me and pushed me toward the door. I didn't have time to react, and found myself being herded out into the hall with everyone else.

"We can explain everything," said Scott.

"No, you can't," replied one of the guards. "Be quiet and start walking."

As we started down the hall, Doug said, "We work for the elevator company."

"No, you don't. We checked. Now we are going to get to the bottom of this." The guard didn't seem very friendly or happy. "We will question you, and then we call the police, and then you will get arrested for trespassing, and breaking into our network, and then you're going to go to jail for a long time."

I glanced over at Scott and Garth. They looked genuinely worried. I remembered that time when I ended up in jail myself. That was not a good time. I didn't want to do that again.

We trudged in silence for only a short while until I overheard one of the guards say, "They must have called for help, and these three showed up."

The first guard then yelled, "Stop!"

We stopped and turned to look. He pointed at Garth and demanded, "Give me your phone."

Garth said, "I'm not really inclined."

The guard waved his gun at Garth, which did a very good job of draining the blood from his face. "We take security very seriously around here." Garth pulled out his phone and handed it over.

Then they turned to Scott. "You, too!"

Scott took his time studying all the men. There were four of them. For a minute I thought he was going to try something, but in the end he handed over his phone, too. I guess he thought it wasn't worth it.

One by one the rest of us handed over our phones, too, first Cheryl, then Doug, then me.

"We may as well do this right here, right now," said the first guard. "Take off your backpacks, too." I groaned, and did as I was told. So did everyone else. "Check their pockets, too."

The guards started slapping our pockets, trying to feel for anything else. Doug had a pocket full of popular generic keys that might fit various things. He lost that.

When it was my turn, the guard slapped my side then gestured with his hand for me to hand it over. I groaned again and pulled out my backup phone. This was the one I used to spy on Smith MacNeil's house. Man! If I've learned anything from situations like this is to always have a backup phone. Now I've lost mine!

"I want to keep my laptop!" said Scott. "It's still in the server room."

"You'll be lucky to keep the shirt on your back."

The guard with Doug's backpack went over to the head guard and showed the open pack to him. The man whistled. "Wow. You were really up to no good, huh? What is all this stuff?" He looked up at Doug, then continued. "I'll tell you what it is. Evidence." He shook his head. "Boy, you're in trouble."

"If you think that's bad," I said, "You should look in mine."

The man eyed me, wondering whether to believe me or not. Then another guard handed him my pack. He opened it and looked in. "What? What's so special in here?"

"Take a look at that folded-up piece of paper."

Scott and Garth looked at me completely confused, but not daring to say anything.

The guard found the paper, opened it, held it up, and read to himself. The expression on his face slowly turned from anger to another kind of anger. While before he had been mad at us for trying to break into his building, now he was angry that we had been given permission to do exactly that by his CEO.

I knew what he was going to say. He was going to give our stuff back and say, "Get out of here!" But he was taking his time. I guess by now saying that was harder than it should have been.

But he never got the words out of his mouth, because just then, from around the corner at the end of the hall, stepped Larry the psychopath, followed by Max, the guy who tried to kill me, followed by Sven, another man who tried to kill me, and who did kill my boss, Victor. It seemed the men from the jailbreak were right here, and suddenly I didn't think we were going to make it out alive.

12:01 AM

While the professional guards may have had boundaries on what they shouldn't do with their weapons, these men did not. As soon as they saw us, Larry yelled, "Shoot!" and they started firing.

I found myself already several strides away when my brain

finally decided that I should start running, and by then it probably couldn't have told me anything else, anyway. It's at times like that when reason and thought themselves become trampled down in the mad rush to get away. Self-preservation really kicks in. I ran fast and took corners. I burst through doors leading to stairwells, and took them two at a time.

I left the guys far behind. I even left Cheryl behind, which bothered me. My brain told me I wouldn't be much help to her if I were dead, but that may have just been an excuse to preserve self. My instincts told me to run to the roof where we came from, but something else told me that's where they would look. So I had to find somewhere new, where I hadn't been before.

I went through the nearest door, and while it was open I could make out a desk. Then I closed the door and hid behind the desk, curling up and welcoming the dark like a blanket over me, a bulletproof blanket, that would magic me away to somewhere else.

But I didn't go anywhere else. I stayed there, seeing nothing, hearing only the beating of my heart, and my lungs slowly returning to normal breathing.

It took a while.

After a while my eyes slowly adjusted. The light from the hall poured in under the door and illuminated the underside of the desk I hid behind. I could make out filing cabinets in the room, and a chair nearby.

Maybe I could make it to the roof. But for what purpose?

If I had a phone I could call for help.

Maybe there was a phone in the room that worked. I slowly crawled out of my hole and tried looking around. I saw in the shadows what looked like a desk phone. I could shine a light at it if I had a phone, but I didn't, so I picked up the receiver, hoping the buttons would illuminate. They didn't. And there was no dial tone. I tried pushing what I thought was the nine, hoping to get an outside line. There was still no dial tone. I pressed everything, but nothing helped. They must have cut the phone lines or the power or something.

I put the phone down, and as I did I heard talking in the hall, and I noticed the light flicker. Someone was outside the room.

I ducked down again and willed with all my heart not to be discovered and killed. It was exhausting.

I heard someone in the hall say, "Alright. I'm on my way back," then the noise went away.

I allowed myself to breathe again, and as I did, I tried to picture God with me. If ever I needed his help it was now. Maybe he could magic me out of this. I imagined him hunched over the desk, holding onto it with one hand. He was saying, "I love you, Jeff."

I said, "I love you too, sir, but is now the time for this? We are in some serious danger here."

He said, "I know you love me, my friend Jeff, and I appreciate it. But do you love your friends too?"

I thought briefly. "Well, not in a romantic way, of course. In a brotherly-love type of way, sure. You know, a normal friendship love, sure."

Our conversation was interrupted by Larry's voice over the PA speaker in the hall. He said, "Oh, Jeff. Jeffery-boy. Jeff Davis. Jeff Davis. I know you can hear me. I know you're out there. But you know who's not out there? All your friends. They're here with me. Scott, Garth, Doug, and even Cheryl. They are keeping me company right here. I could go out and get you, too, but I had a thought. We could do something else. We could play a little game."

12:37 AM

Larry's voice continued over the speakers. "Before we

begin the game, Jeff, let me introduce you to the contestants."

As I sat huddled under the desk in the dark, I hoped he was bluffing. He didn't have anyone there with him.

"First, and perhaps most important to you, is the woman you love, Cheryl Bankowsky. Say 'Hello', Cheryl." There was a pause, then I heard Cheryl's voice say, "Hi, Jeff."

I didn't like the feelings inside of me that were welling up. I didn't like them at all, but before I could wrap my mind around what I was feeling, Larry continued. "Next is your friend, Scott Stark. Say 'Hello', Scott."

Scott's voice continued immediately, "Run, Jeff! Get out out of here! Hurry!" His words were cut short by the sound of physical violence and groaning.

"We may hear from Scott again later, after he recovers, but first we want to say hello to Garth Fonte. I'm sure he's dying to talk to you. Oh, Jeff, since you can't see this, I should tell you that Garth's knees are literally shaking. And his face is pale. Say something, Garth, if you can." I could make out Garth's weak voice squeak out the word, "Hi." It wasn't "Greetings", or "Good evening to you." It was just a simple, "Hi." He sounded terrified.

"And finally we have Doug Grimm. You didn't tell me, Jeff, that Doug knows how to fight. He's a bit scratched up, and so are a few of my guys. He fought well, but I won in the end. I win every time. I always have, and I always will. It's time for you to say 'Hi' to Jeff, Doug. And for the sake of my own entertainment, I hope you refuse, just so we can have a bit more fun with you." There was a very short pause, but I clearly heard Doug say, "Hello." He was breathing hard.

"The game is this, Jeff. I'm going to take one of these contestants here, and start beating on their head with a blunt object. I will stop the beating when you come out of hiding. The game is to see how long you will last. Now, who will I pick? The woman? No, that's the oldest trope in the book. What do you take me for? But then whom? Scott? Maybe, but you are good friends, and I don't want to make it too easy on you. That leaves Doug and Garth." Then I heard Larry barking out orders. "You, put him down on the floor here. You and you, hold him down. You, get me a chair."

I turned to God. "What do I do?" I pleaded.

He looked into my eyes with love and compassion. "Do you love your friends?"

"If I go there, they're going to kill me."

"Do you love them?"

"Will you promise me I won't get hurt?"

He shook his head, "No."

"Well, Cheryl keeps saying I'm not going to die yet."

"She might be mistaken."

"What, are you leading me to my death? Do you want me to die?"

"There is no greater love than to lay down your life for your friends. I gave up my life for you on the cross. You also, can give up your life for your friends."

As I stared back into the eyes of God, I heard Larry say, "You'll find us in the basement cafe."

There was a dull thud, and Garth cried out in pain. Larry yelled, "One!"

There was another thud, and Garth cried out again. "Two!"

Another thud. "Three!" This time I heard many voices join in on the count. The room must be full.

I whispered to God, "Is Garth going to die?"

"If you don't intervene, yes."

"If I go there, will I save his life?"

He slowly nodded. "Yes."

I scrambled up from behind the desk, out the door, and ran down the hall as fast as I could.

CHAPTER 19

12:45 AM

As I hurried through the building, I could hear Larry call out numbers. At the beginning, I heard Garth yell each time. But after a few, the sharp cries turned to moaning, and then I couldn't hear him at all. At one point I heard Cheryl scream, "Stop it Larry! Stop it! You're killing him!" I ran faster.

I finally made it down the basement level, and ran around to the right hallway. I could see a tough-looking man standing near the door. He stepped aside to let me in.

I was breathing hard when I ran through the doorway into the room where everybody was assembled. As I did so, I yelled "Stop!!"

Then I stood and looked around. Cheryl was being held while standing there. Her eyes were wide with distress. Scott and Doug were both on the ground with several guys on top of them. It looked like they had been struggling.

Garth lay on the floor, or perhaps his body lay on the floor. His head was covered in red. I didn't see him breathing.

Larry stood there, looking at me, breathing a little hard himself. He had stopped counting. He didn't seem angry. He wasn't even happy. He said, "Ah. You could actually hear me. I was beginning to wonder." He tossed the chair he was holding off to the side. It was red, too. "You know what your problem is, Jeff?"

"I care?"

"Yes! Yes, that's it exactly! You care. You care about 'justice', whatever that means. I don't even know what 'justice' means. 'The law' is simply a set of rules that some arbitrary people make, and for some reason you think you need to do what they say. Ridiculous!

"They're elected. They have the authority to make laws."

"Elected?! Ha! What does that mean? All that means is they have the support of the majority. And what is that worth? Nothing. If all your friends jumped off a bridge, would you jump off too? No, your mother taught you that when you were young. You actually shouldn't follow the majority, because the majority is usually wrong. A good investor will look to see how everyone else is investing and do the opposite. So don't give me this rubbish about following the majority. If everybody thinks something is wrong, it's probably a good idea."

"There are moral laws. Some things are just wrong, like murder."

"Moral laws are just what society tells you you're supposed to do, without writing it down, like you're supposed to not put your elbows on the table."

"No, moral laws come from God."

"God is just a made-up concept to keep you under the control of the religious leaders. Instead of society telling you what you're not supposed to do, the religious leaders tell you what you're not supposed to do. They're just as wrong. In fact, they are the enemy, Jeff."

I didn't have anything to say to that, so he continued. "But a few of us have managed to pull away from the grasp of society, and like a rocket escaping the gravity of Earth, I have escaped the pull of society. I write my own laws. I live by my own standards. I am the only one here who is truly free."

"You're not free!" We all turned to Cheryl, who shouted it. "You're in pain. You're wounded. You're a hurting man who is fighting back at everyone who hurt you first. But it doesn't have to be this way. You can forgive and live at peace."

"Cheryl," Larry began. "What are you talking about?"

"Your parents. They must have done terrible things to you for you to do what you did to them."

"My parents?" Larry slowly approached Cheryl. "My parents were the most loving, kind, compassionate, giving, serving people you could ever meet." He pointed at Max's gun and gestured for it. Max handed it over, and Larry held it and kept walking around.

"Then why did you... how could you..."

"Kill them? Haven't you heard anything I just said? When I first understood that society's rules were not to my benefit, but actually weighed me down like a wet blanket, I determined to free myself completely from them. It started with a little stomping on the neighbor's garden, then stealing things and throwing them away, then bigger and bigger acts of freedom, until one day I knew what I had to do. There was one test in front of me, and I knew that it was my final exam, so to speak. If I could pass that, I would be forever free."

He looked around the room, waiting for someone to ask him what it was. After hearing a random, "Yeah", come from the crowd, he continued.

"If society tells you anything, it's that you're supposed to respond with kindness to people who love you, and in fact it is hard not to. It is the greatest test. If a little girl offers you her last cookie, can you respond by slapping her? If your boss appreciates you and gives you a big raise, can you key his car? If Jesus Christ dies on a cross for you, can you spit in his face? If your parents love you, can you respond by bludgeoning them to death? Well I passed the test!"

"You're crazy!" Cheryl sputtered.

"Am I? I've thought about it, and it all seems very logical to me. And if you think about it, it should make sense to you, too."

Now Larry turned to me. "Jeff, I was going to blow you up in your car, but something Veronica said made me stop. I realized you would be dead, and wouldn't know why I had killed you. But now I'll tell you. It's because of your weakness. It's because of love. Ever since Jade started working with Omniscient, you've been doing selfless things. You got involved in other people's business. You messed up Jade's business. You messed up Yash Nagi's business. And the worst part was you thought you got away with it. But you didn't. You didn't, Jeff. Being good never pays. Love is the greatest weakness, and it cost you your life. Just look! Garth is already dead. You thought you could save him, but instead coming out of hiding to save him cost you your life, too! Stupid! Stupid! Love is never good for you. You only end up dying." Then he held up the gun to me, and shot me in the chest.

12:52 AM

By the time his arm came up and the bullet started its journey toward my unprotected body, my adrenaline had time to kick in, but I didn't have time to do anything about it. I felt not only the bullet pierce my chest, but also the flesh around the entry point absorb the shock waves. When I looked down to confirm my fears that I had indeed been shot, I noticed a spot on my shirt, and red liquid starting to come out.

I was concerned that the liquid was coming out too fast, so I put my hand over the wound. It didn't do much to stop the flow. By then I noticed I had trouble breathing, so I coughed a few times and was startled by the blood spraying out of my mouth. Now I was concerned that I not only might die from heart failure, but from my lungs filling up and downing me.

By then I was on the floor. I could hear Cheryl screaming, which saddened me, because I didn't want to leave her. I wanted to stay, and protect her, and love her, but now I couldn't, because I was dying. I felt so sad for her, and for our future together that will now never exist.

But maybe I could survive if I could only keep on breathing. I tried to lie on my side, holding myself up on my elbow, just so that the blood wouldn't drain into my lungs and kill me. If I could just keep on breathing, I would survive. But it took too much energy to keep myself up, so I collapsed onto my back.

All I had to do was to survive until an ambulance showed up, but then I remembered that no ambulance was coming. And my friends couldn't do anything for me. And I couldn't do anything for myself. So I cried out to God to save me, but the liquid kept me from speaking clearly, so I prayed in my mind until I ran out of energy to even try to breathe.

I lay on my back, not breathing, wondering what was going on, but knowing exactly what was going on. I was dying, and I might already be dead. For a moment I stopped being concerned with my immediate surroundings and considered everything else in life, at least the important things.

I was thankful for all the years that my mom took care of me by herself. My relationship with my dad was never good, but lately it had started improving, which made me glad. I should have spent more time with him. I thought of Cheryl. I did love her, and was hoping to spend the rest of my life with her, but even still I was glad for the time I did get with her. It was good time. I even enjoyed hanging out with my friends from work. Yeah, I should have put more effort into those relationships, too. And then there was God.

But before I could ponder that, I found myself sitting up and looking around. I could see and hear everything with total clarity, in fact better than normal. I could hear the fluorescent lights hum loudly in the ceiling. I could make out the smell of Cheryl's tears, and Garth's blood. I could feel the slight bumps in the flooring I was sitting on. Every shade and hue of color was unique and distinct to me. And I had so much energy inside of me. I hesitated to believe I was dead, because I felt so alive. I jumped to my feet.

I saw Scott and Doug, still pinned down, clearly distraught. I saw Cheryl, fighting and struggling to come to me. I tried to tell her that I was OK, but she didn't seem to notice. Then she did break free, and came rushing over to me, but not directly to me. She approached the floor, which caused me to look down at the floor. What I saw shocked me. It was my dead body, lying there motionless. I was so startled, that I jumped up and stepped off to the side, watching the action from a few feet away.

That's when I noticed the two other men with me, one on my left, and one on my right. They looked like men, but had a strange glow about them. I was about to ask them who they were, but instead they took me by the arms and lifted me straight up. We flew straight through the building, up into the dark sky, through the clouds, then soon I could see the Earth below us. I blinked a few times as we traveled across the expanse of the universe, and soon arrived on a grassy knoll. The two men set me down, and then vanished.

I looked around me. The grass was the greenest, most lush lawn I had ever seen. The sky was the most brilliant and dazzling azure. The few wisps of white clouds in the sky looked as beautifully set in their backdrop of blue as any painting I had ever seen on Earth. It took my breath away. The only thing I didn't see on this sunny day was the sun.

But soon the source of the light came walking up the hill in front of me.

* * *

On Earth, I would have squinted at his glory, but here I

took it all in with eyes wide. His hair was white as wool. His robes radiated energy as if just being close to the one wearing them made them glow. He may have had sandals on and a sash around his chest, but I didn't notice because what really got my attention was his eyes. They were like pools of eternity, as if they were windows to ancient times and also future times, that held all secrets of everything that ever was and all that was to come. And they smiled at me.

He walked up to me, and as I stood there, not knowing what to do, or if I should or could do anything, he embraced me with his strong arms and said softly, "Welcome home."

I was like a child, and like a child, I threw my short arms as far around my papa as I could reach. Then I stayed there for a long time, resting in his warmth, feeling his heartbeat and his breath upon me.

Eventually we let go and he held me at arm's length and said, "I knew you'd make it back."

Confused, I said, "Back?"

He smiled warmly and explained. "Your physical body was born on Earth and is of Earth. Your spirit came from me." He pointed to his heart. "And now you are back."

I pondered this idea, and finally decided that it made sense. Humans on Earth do sort of fit in on that planet, but sort of don't. We are a little like the animals, but in more ways like this one in front of me. I said, "It's good to be here."

He said, "It's a wonderful place, here with me. It's full of peace and joy and excitement. You'll have a lot of fun. We'll have a lot of fun together." He winked.

I smiled back.

"I've been working on a house for you."

"For me?"

"Yes. Everyone needs a place to call home. You're going to like yours. But of course you will, because I know exactly what you like." He grinned and poked me in the chest with a finger.

"And I've been working on all those things. And I've had help."

I laughed, as if this one needed help from anyone. "Who's helping you?"

"It's not that I need help. I enjoy working together with my children. He's Victor Akulov, your former boss."

I paused, but he continued. "Don't worry, here he's a nice guy. He's very friendly and kind."

"That doesn't really sound like him."

He laughed, and when he did, his laughter stirred up the wind into happy gusts and the blades of grass fluttered with joy. I felt it, too. He said, "That sounds exactly like Victor, the Victor I made him to be, the Victor he always wanted to be himself. Now he finally is."

I thought of anyone else here I might know. "Is Garth here too?"

He shook his head. "No, not yet."

"But it looked like…"

He interrupted me. "Yes, it looked like it, but it turns out your cranium can take more abuse than you thought it could. Garth will survive."

"A full recovery?"

"He may have some scars, but as a result he will lose a lot of his pride, which is a good thing. You'll enjoy working with him."

I didn't understand. "You mean when he finally gets here?"

"Your house is not yet finished, Jeff."

I thought of all the pain and hurt and injustice and evil still going on down there on Earth. I didn't want to be part of that again. I was just getting used to this new world. I said, "But why?"

Instead of responding with words, he motioned with his hand at the ground. The grass faded away to reveal a window to Earth that opened up on the room where my dead body lay.

He said, "Because Cheryl is praying."

* * *

I saw Cheryl kneeling beside me, one hand bawled up, the other pointing at the sky. Her face was wet with tears, but she wasn't defeated. She was fighting. I heard her declare, "You promised! You promised!" She was looking up at us. "You promised me in a dream! You showed me we would be married. You showed me our children. You promised!"

It felt very strange for my best friend to be so vexed while I felt nothing but overwhelming peace all through my being.

I looked from Cheryl to the one next to me. He was watching this unconventional prayer with seriousness. I dared to interrupt and ask, "What dream?"

He said, "I gave her a dream about her future. She will share it with you in good time."

"That's why she was always so sure I wouldn't die yet."

He nodded.

"So what happens now?"

"Now I'm sending you back."

I sighed.

"But before I do, there are things you need. Jeff, my friend, you may ask me for help."

I responded with, "Uh... like what?"

"First of all, your body is broken. Your chest has a bullet in it, your heart is ruptured, and your lungs of full of blood. You wouldn't enjoy going back to that."

"Can you fix that?"

He grinned, then waved his hand over the window on the ground, which showed a close-up x-ray of my body. With a wiggle of his pinky, the lungs cleared up, the heart repaired, and the bullet disappeared. "I'll let the skin heal itself. The scar will be a reminder of my power to heal."

"Um... that's a bit ironic, isn't it?"

He smiled. "I don't mind a bit of irony. Isn't it also ironic that if you want to save your life you will lose it, but if you lose your life for my sake you will find it?"

"Um... I guess so."

"What else do you need?"

"You're asking me?"

He nodded. "Yes. Think about the situation. What else can I give you?"

I thought for a moment, then said, "Well, if nobody is paying attention to me, maybe I could call the police if I had a phone."

He turned back to the window and wiped his hand from one side to the other. The picture shifted fast in reverse, as if he hit a rewind button. The scene in front of us now was of Scott and me at the police station.

I heard the detective say, "If I discover anything, I'll let you know. Your email address is still the same?"

I, in the vision, said, "Yes."

Then Scott grinned and said, "But he keeps breaking his phone."

I saw myself rolling my eyes and replied, "It's not me who keeps breaking it."

"Tell you what." Scott reached into his pocket and took out his smartphone. "You can have mine."

Then I remembered! I gasped in surprise and looked up. "Scott gave me his old phone! I put it into that other pocket of my pants and forgot about it!"

The one next to me smiled and said, "Yes."

"Wow. Thanks!"

"My pleasure, Jeff. What else do you need?"

I thought some more. "Do you want to give me the Wi-Fi password? If I can get onto that network, maybe I can access Security Tight and get video of my murder for the police. Wow, that sounds weird. And Omniscient's data back."

He smiled and moved his hand again.

I said, "What? We're going to time travel to where I learned the password? I'm pretty sure I don't actually know it."

He grinned as the video stopped at Daryl Bankowsky's house. I watched Daryl ask his friend Bob, "Do you remember in University when we found that empty broom closet?"

"Of course I remember," replied Robert Alexander, the CEO of FutureTech, "We studied there, and ate there, and hid from the authorities there. We called it our bastion."

Daryl said, "Yes! Bastion. I remember that name."

I looked up and said, "The password is 'Bastion'? He named it after their hide-out?"

The one with me nodded, then said with a grin, "All lowercase, no spaces."

These were very valuable gifts I was being given. I said, "Thank you."

"Anything else?"

"Um... yeah. In the room, all eyes are on me. Can you move the action somewhere else?"

He snapped his fingers and the view was back to the present. He said to Cheryl, "Go." Cheryl got up, and started walking toward Larry.

Then I noticed I was off the ground and approaching the scene. Halfway there, I turned around in mid-air and said, "Wait! If I'm not going to die before I get married and have children, does that mean I'm invincible until then? I'll have... what's the term? Plot armor?"

I heard him say, "Will you always have someone praying for you like that?"

Oh. That was a good question, but before I had time to ponder it, everything went black, and I was lying on a cold floor.

Then my heart started beating again.

CHAPTER 20

12:56 AM

As I lay there with my eyes closed, I waited for the right time to make my move.

I could hear Cheryl in a direct verbal confrontation with Larry. She said, "Jeff was a hundred times a better man than you!"

Larry laughed out loud. "In what way?"

"He cared! He was good! He wanted the world to be a better place. He worked hard to make it a better place."

"Weaknesses!"

"He wanted to save Garth! He came here and risked his own life to save his friend's life."

"That's the exact opposite of what you're supposed to do. He got an F for that one."

"No, Larry, that's where you're wrong. By your own definition, Jeff won and you lost."

Larry paused slightly, then said, "What are you talking about?"

"Don't you always say to not follow what society tells you to do?"

"Of course."

"And if the world tells you to do something, you should do the opposite?"

"Probably."

"And if everyone says you must absolutely, definitely, do this one thing, then only the lowest of fools does it?"

"Yeah."

"Well, what bigger message does the world give you than to 'Look out for number one'? 'What's in it for me?' 'Self care' 'Self love' 'Get the biggest piece of the pie.'"

"Shut up."

But Cheryl continued. "If there is any message coming from society, it's that you need to run away from death, not toward it. Jeff ran toward it. He died. He gave up his life. And you saved yours."

"Shut up."

"Good for you, Larry! Larry saved his own life, just like everybody else in the world. The world tells you to keep on living, so you did, Larry. You lived, just like you're supposed to. Good for you! Jeff came running toward the bullet, something you wouldn't dream of doing in a million years!"

"I said, 'Shut up'. I can do anything I want to."

"No you can't! You're a slave to life just like everybody else. Life is your master, and you are its slave. Your master, life, says you must run away from the bullet, not toward it, and you say, 'Yes, master! I am your slave and will do whatever you want.'"

Then I heard a gunshot, and I opened my eyes to see what happened. Nothing happened, but Larry with gun pointed up, looked very disturbed. He was probably just trying to regain control of the conversation. I closed my eyes again.

Larry spoke. "I am a slave to nobody. I can do anything I want to. I can do things that other people can't, and certainly everything Jeff can do. I'll show you. I'll show you all."

I heard gasps and murmurings around the room, so I took a peek to see what was going on. Larry had the gun to his own head.

He said, "Let it be known that I, the greatest of all,

conquered even death itself. Well done, Mikey Christopher. Well done, Larry Trilbert. Well done, Steven McDonald. Well done, Vesuvius." That's the last thing he ever said.

1:01 AM

When I heard the gunshot, I knew that was my queue to act. I reached into my lower pants pocket and pulled out Scott's old phone and quickly dialed 911. When it connected, I sat up and said loudly, "911? I know where all the inmates are hiding. They're in the basement of the FutureTech building. Send the police immediately."

When the bad guys with guns saw their boss dead, and me come back to life, and knowing the police were on their way, it didn't take them long to decide to run away as fast as they could. For a moment, Max looked like he wanted to point a gun at me, but his was gone, so instead he just ran with everyone else.

In their rush to leave, I added into the phone, "And send an ambulance. Or two."

Cheryl came running to me and hugged me and started crying uncontrollably.

Then I gave Scott's phone back to him and said, "Try connecting using the password 'bastion'. All lower case, no spaces."

Doug went over to Garth's body and started CPR. Pretty soon he called out, "I think there's a heartbeat." We all breathed a little better after that.

Scott said, "The password worked. We're in."

I said, "Try to connect to Security Tight. If you can, it would be great to make sure all doors are locked, once they're outside, so those guys can't come back for hostages."

He nodded, then soon he smiled. "It's working." Then soon he said, "They're outside, and the doors are locked. And I'm watching video of the outside cameras. There are flashing lights. The police came fast. Um..."

"What is it?" I asked.

"There appears to be a shoot-out. Max is on the ground, and he's not moving. A bunch of guys are down. Now I see hands going up. The rest of them are surrendering."

"We may as well open the doors again if it's safe."

"Yeah. Done." Then he pointed his finger at me. "You have some explaining to do." But instead of waiting for a reply, he went to check on Garth. He bent down and put a hand on his friend. "Hang on, buddy! An ambulance is on its way. Help is coming. Hang on!"

Doug paused his CPR and looked for signs of life, then announced, "Garth is breathing on his own."

A wave of relief rippled through my body. I hugged Cheryl even tighter.

Then paramedics burst through the door. One guy went over to Larry's body and shook his head. "He's gone."

Another went to Garth and immediately checked for signs of life. Then he waved over the others carrying a stretcher. As they were coming, he asked about Garth, "What happened to him?"

Doug said, "Repeated blows to the head... with that chair." He pointed to a chair lying on the floor stained with blood.

As they were taking Doug away on the stretcher, Cheryl called out, "Is he going to be OK?"

We heard Garth's weak voice reply, "Affirmative, Ms. Bankowsky," which made us smile.

As I finally pulled myself off the floor into a standing position, the last paramedic looked at me and said, "You look hurt."

Scott said, "He got shot in the chest."

That made the guy look very concerned, so I had to calm him down. "I'm feeling very good, though, so I think I'll just walk. See?" I walked back and forth for him, so he could see me do it.

He frowned. "You still need to come in to the hospital."

"Fine," I said. "I need to go there, anyway."

"Good. I'll go get another stretcher for him." He nodded at the body, then left.

That left the four of us standing around in silence, then Cheryl said, "Can we leave this room, please?"

As we walked out the door and down the hall, I said, "So, I guess I'll head out to the hospital. How about you guys?"

"I'm coming with you," said Cheryl.

"Now that we have access to the network," said Scott, "I want to get our encryption key, so we can start recovering our data."

Doug nodded. "I think it'll work. I'll help you with that."

"Thanks."

We stopped by the guards' room to retrieve our laptops and phones. Then Scott and Doug went one way, probably towards the server room, and Cheryl and I went the other way.

Cheryl and I held hands in silence until we got to the main doors, where there was still a bustle of activity. We managed to walk past them without being stopped. Then we held hands again outside in the darkness as we walked away from the building.

"Ah, where are we going?" Cheryl asked. "We don't have a car."

"Maybe there's a bus stop around here somewhere."

"I think you just feel like going for a walk."

I shrugged.

"And talk? You could tell me what happened to you."

So as we strolled around the city, in search of a bus stop, I tried to explain to my best friend what happened to me. When I was done, I asked her to explain to me about the dream God had given her.

Then it was her turn to talk as I listened.

When she was done, we both received a text message at

the same time. It was from Cheryl's mom, saying Dad was awake.

I said, "Let's go to the hospital."

"At this time of the night?"

I nodded. "Yup."

She chuckled and said, "OK. But you need to change or put on a jacket or something, because you're still covered in blood."

I nodded. "Good idea."

2:33 AM

We arrived at the hospital with the intention of visiting no less than three people, but before we saw any of them, someone else approached us first.

The man pointed at me and said, "You left the scene before giving a statement." It was Detective Wakefield.

I shrugged. "I just wanted to get out of there."

"You can stop by the station in the morning. That's usually how you end up doing these things."

I nodded. "OK, I'll do it."

"They say you got shot, but here you are."

I shrugged, not knowing what to say. Where would I even start?

He continued. "You got lucky, kid. It must have been a defective bullet–not enough powder–enough to touch you, but not enough to do damage."

"God is with him, Detective," said Cheryl.

"I'll say!" he continued. "And speaking of doing damage, the gunshots inflicted to your buddies Max and Sven at the shoot-out were fatal. You no longer need to be concerned about them."

"They're dead?" asked Cheryl.

"Dead as dead."

I felt myself relax and I could breathe easier. "Detective..." I began.

"Yeah?"

"Just before Larry... killed himself... he said good-bye to his aliases, presumably himself."

"You see this is the kind of thing I'm looking forward to hearing in your statement. Who did he list in his goodbye?"

"Um... Mikey Christopher, Larry Trilbert, Steven McDonald, and lastly, Vesuvius."

"Really? No kidding? Vesuvius? He called himself Vesuvius."

I shrugged. "Yeah."

"And he was serious?"

I nodded.

He rubbed his chin and said, "Well, would you look at that. That would explain why everyone else was so easily under his control. He already was their boss. Well, if that's the case, kid, you really don't have any enemies left, do you? You're a free man!"

I nodded, not knowing the words to say, and being too choked up to say anything. Cheryl squeezed my hand.

"Stop by tomorrow and we'll get your full testimony." He pointed at Cheryl. "You, too."

Joseph slapped my shoulder on his way past me, then turned back and said, "Oh, you should have told us the jailbirds locked up the real security guards in a back room. They were there a long time before we found them."

I was stunned. "I had no idea."

He waved his hand back at me. "Go to bed," he said, then walked away, leaving Cheryl and me to find the people we really came here for.

2:50 AM

The nurses wouldn't let us see Garth or Smith MacNeil–
something about visiting hours–but they assured us that they
were both fine and would both make complete recoveries.

But they let us see Cheryl's dad, because we were family,
which was close enough to be true. We came in holding hands,
and Cheryl called him her dad, so they just let me in, too.
Technically I wasn't family yet.

When we went through the doors, Cheryl's dad was in bed
with his eyes closed and her mom was sitting on a chair with
her head leaning against the wall. But when she saw us, she got
up and gave each of us a hug with a smile on her face.

"How's Dad?" Cheryl whispered.

"He's fine! He's doing great. But he's sleeping, so let's be
quiet."

"Why would I want to sleep when my favorite daughter is
here?" We looked and saw Daryl with his eyes open and
smiling at us.

Cheryl cried, "Daddy!" and gave him a big hug in bed.

I shook his hand awkwardly and mumbled, "I'm glad
you're better."

"I am better, Jeff. But I've heard that things have been
happening while I was out."

I nodded. "The office was bombed. But nobody was hurt,
much."

"And now Future Tech doesn't have a CEO," he added with
sadness in his eyes. "And I wasn't around to help the board
pick a new one. I own some of that company, you know."

"No, I didn't know. They picked Larry, our security
consultant."

He frowned. "Don't you mean Steven McDonald?"

"Same guy. He went by a few names. It turns out he was a
psychopath. And a crime boss."

Daryl shook his head. "It seems Future Tech could use

some real leadership. Now that I'm back, I can help out."

"Are you saying you'll be the next CEO?"

"No, probably not. But maybe Peter can help out in the meantime. Omniscient needs a new place to set up shop, at least temporarily. Maybe you can move into Future Tech's building."

"Like merging the companies?"

"No, I don't think so. But maybe the companies can be... friends."

I smiled. That might work.

My phone suddenly made a noise like a twiggersnakle, and I was going to just ignore it, until I remembered that this particular twiggersnakle sound came from our Omniscient software that recently got hacked. Could it be? I quickly checked, and sure enough, I had just received a message from Scott that said, "Pop pop popsicle. Ice ice icicle. Test test testing... testing... If this works, Omniscient is back up."

I smiled and said out loud, "Hey! The guys got Omniscient back up and running!"

"That's great!" said Cheryl.

"Wonderful news!" said Daryl.

I quickly typed something into my phone, and held it for Daryl to read. When he did, his eyebrows shot up in surprise. Then he smiled at me. Then he nodded his head, and reached out to shake my hand, which I did. Then I announced, "Well, it's late. Have a good night, everyone. Cheryl, I'll drive you home."

"OK."

On our way out of the building, instead of turning to the left to go to the parking lot, I held her hand and turned right.

"Where are we going?" she asked.

"There's one more thing I want to do."

3:13 AM

Cheryl and I sat snuggled together on a wooden bench in the little garden beside the Hospital building, the soft glow of an old-fashioned lamp post smiling down on us.

Trying to be romantic, I said, "I like you, Cheryl."

She smiled and replied, "I like you too, Jeff."

"I've really enjoyed being your friend. You're my best friend, Cheryl."

"And you're mine."

"Well," I paused. "I think I'm God's friend too. Or maybe he is mine."

She chuckled. "You may have two best friends, as long as he is one and I'm the other."

I nodded. "Good. Then you're one of my best friends."

She laughed again.

"And I love you very much," I said, patting my pocket to make sure that the certain something was still there. "But I want to be more than friends."

She pulled her head back, and looked at me without saying anything.

I continued. "Um... so... ah..." Suddenly feeling nervous, I pulled out the little box from my pocket and opened it, to remind me of what I was doing.

Cheryl pulled her hands to her face.

Repositioning myself to place one knee on the ground in front of the bench, I held the little box up to her and asked her a question.

She nodded in agreement, then said, "Yes!" Then feeling much too energetic for this time of the night, she got up and jumped a little. Then we hugged. And we kissed a little, too.

Then Cheryl tried on the ring, which fit pretty well. She took many pictures from every possible angle and sent them to all her friends and family.

We didn't get a lot of responses right away, because people

were asleep of course, but we did get one from Cheryl's dad.

It said, "Congratulations, daughter! Congratulations, son!"

And in that moment, I remembered how I grew up broken, without a dad, never thinking in my wildest dreams I would ever feel whole inside again.

But now I was.

I took a deep breath and let it out, as a tear trickled down my cheek. Cheryl saw it, wiped it away, and asked, "Jeff, are you OK?"

I nodded. "Yeah. Yeah, I am."

The End.

"Servants are cheap.
Friends are expensive.
Sons are priceless."
- Rick Joyner